Love in Chaos

A Platinum Chocolate Psychological Saga

By

LongTemple

Loved in Chaos – A Platinum Chocolate Psychological Saga

This is a work of fiction. Names, characters, businesses, places, events, and incidents are either the product of the author's imagination or used fictitiously. Any resemblance to actual persons, living or dead, or actual events is purely coincidental.

Published by Platinum Chocolate Publishing

An Independent Imprint of LongTemple

ISBN: 978-1-972217-24-5 (paperback)

Cover Design: LongTemple

Interior Layout: LongTemple

First Edition

Printed in the United States of America

10 9 8 7 6 5 4 3 2 1

Dedication

To the version of me who had to make sense of love
without ever being taught what it was supposed to feel like.

To those who were loved—
but not always in ways that felt safe.

To those who learned to survive
before they learned to be.

And to every reader who is still learning how to live beyond what shaped them — this story is for you.

With love,

— LongTemple

Table of Contents

Chapter One: Loved in Chaos

The first thing Kia ever understood about the world was not language, not faces, not even love in the way most children come to know it—it was atmosphere.

The kind that shifted without warning and settled into her body before she had words to explain what she was feeling.

She learned early that a room could carry emotion the way the air carried sound, that something unseen could press against her chest, tighten her breathing, and still her without instruction.

Before she could form full sentences, she already knew how to listen with her entire body—how to read the space between voices, how to recognize when something was about to change without needing it to be named.

By the time the world slowed down in 2020, that instinct had never left her. New York had always been a city layered in motion, noise resting on top of noise until silence felt imagined rather than experienced. But now the streets held something different. Sirens still passed, but no longer in constant chorus.

Conversations no longer spilled endlessly onto sidewalks. The rhythm had softened, as if the city itself had been forced to inhale and hold it, and in that held breath Kia felt something familiar settle into her body in a way that made her uneasy.

Because quiet, for her, had never been neutral. It lived in her shoulders, in the slight lift of her chest, in the way her body prepared before anything had happened. It carried anticipation—the kind that did not announce itself but made space for what might come next.

Still, she stepped into the park, her movement slow and deliberate, composed in a way that had taken years to learn, not as performance but as control.

Her beauty did not announce itself loudly, but it carried presence. Her skin held a soft, luminous cream tone beneath natural light, and her hair, thick and jet black, fell with controlled fullness, framing her face and settling with quiet weight against her back.

Her features reflected both inheritance and contradiction—almond-shaped eyes that observed more than they revealed, full lips that softened her expression without weakening it, a structure that felt both delicate and grounded.

She looked like someone who understood how to exist without offering everything she carried, and what no one could see was how early that understanding had been learned.

Her mother had been the kind of woman people noticed immediately—not because she demanded attention, but because she held it without effort. A petite Chinese woman with a frame so slight it seemed almost fragile, she carried a beauty that was precise and striking, porcelain skin stretched smooth across high cheekbones, her dark eyes sharp and expressive in ways that could invite or cut depending on the moment.

She could be radiant, fully present, laughing in a way that filled a room with warmth, her presence expansive and bright.

And then, without warning, that warmth could disappear, replaced by something faster, sharper, harder to follow, as if the emotional ground beneath her had shifted and taken the room with it.

Her moods did not transition. They turned.

For Kia, that meant learning that love could arrive full and real and shift just as quickly into something she could not steady herself against.

Her mother was not absent, not distant, not uncaring—she was present in a way that was intense and consuming, but not consistent, and that inconsistency became something Kia adapted to before she ever questioned it.

Her father existed in contrast so complete it felt intentional. A tall Black man, broad-shouldered and grounded, he carried a steadiness that did not need to be announced.

He worked for Con Edison as a licensed electrician and practiced plumber—a man who understood systems, how things connected, how pressure built, how failure happened, and how to restore what could be restored.

At home, he moved with that same understanding. He did not rush. He did not raise his voice to compete. Where her mother's energy shifted, he steadied. He did not try to overpower chaos—he contained what he could and protected what mattered.

And in that consistency, Kia learned something her body would carry long before she ever found language for it—that stability, even when it does not fix everything, is a form of love.

Kia was born between them, not as a compromise but as a convergence of everything they were and everything they could not fully reconcile. Even as a child, there was something contained about her—not closed, not rigid, but aware, as if she understood more than she should at that age.

The first memory that stayed with her fully came wrapped in celebration, which made the shift inside it harder to name.

It was Halloween.

Outside, the city moved with joy—children's voices rising and overlapping, costumes brushing past each other, laughter echoing through streets that felt closer in the dark.

Music drifted through open windows and passing cars, old-school R&B grounding everything in something familiar and continuous.

Inside the apartment, the energy did not match.

Her mother moved through the space quickly, her small frame carrying a restless sharpness that filled the room faster than her body should have been able to. *"It's fine, everything is fine,"* she said, her tone bright but edged in a way that did not settle.

Kia sat on the floor, her hands sticky with chocolate, her plastic pumpkin tipped beside her, wrappers clinging to her fingers.

She did not look up immediately because she had already learned that looking was not always the fastest way to understand what was happening.

She listened instead, her body stilling as her breathing adjusted in small, unconscious shifts.

When the knock came, it landed hard against the door. Then again—louder, more insistent.

The room shifted.

Her father stood, his movement unhurried but intentional, his presence creating just enough distance between what was happening and what could happen next.

As he passed her, his hand rested briefly against her head—warm, steady, grounding in a way that required no explanation.

When he opened the door, two uniformed officers stood in the hallway.

"We received a call. Noise disturbance. Possible domestic issue."

Kia did not understand the words, but she understood the change that followed them—the way her mother's energy spiked, the way her voice lifted again, brighter now but tighter underneath.

"There's no problem here," her mother said quickly.

"Everything is under control," her father said, not defensively, not dismissively—simply stating what he intended to be true.

Kia watched from the floor, her body still, absorbing what would later become the foundation of how she understood conflict, presence, and protection.

She did not need to know why the officers were there to understand that something in the room required holding.

And her father held it.

That was the first time she understood—not in words, not in thought, but in the quiet way her body carried it forward—that presence could shape what happened before it ever became what it might have been.

And even now, years later, in a city that had learned how to quiet itself in ways that did not feel natural, she could still feel the echo of that night—not as something pulling her backward, but as something that had followed her forward, waiting to be understood differently.

Chapter Two: The Night the City Wore Masks

By the time she learned how to stay present inside those echoes, they no longer arrived as something that took from her, but as something she could feel fully without disappearing inside of it.

The music did not end so much as it resolved, the final note settling into the quiet with the same patience Ajah brought to everything he touched. His hands lingered over the keys—not because he needed to finish, but because he understood that sound, like emotion, should be allowed to land before anything else began.

Kia sat beside him on the grass, her body still carrying what had passed through her—but not overwhelmed by it. That was the difference now. Not the absence of memory, but her ability to remain present while it moved.

Ajah closed the fallboard gently. *"You stayed with that one longer."*

Kia let out a soft breath. *"Yeah. It didn't feel like it was pulling me under this time."*

"That's because you didn't fight it."

She glanced at him, a faint, knowing look crossing her face. *"You've been saying that for a while."*

He allowed himself a small smile. *"And you've been arguing with me for just as long."*

There was ease in that exchange—the kind that had already been built over time.

Kia leaned back slightly on her hands, her shoulders loosening as she allowed herself to settle fully into where she was. *"I'm not arguing anymore. I think I'm just… catching up."*

Ajah turned his head toward her. *"That's different."*

"It feels different."

He stood then, collapsing the stand and securing the instrument with practiced ease. There was no performance in the way he handled his piano—just familiarity, repetition, and care.

Kia rose as well, brushing her hands lightly against her coat, her body already anticipating the movement that would follow.

She had watched him do this enough times to know the rhythm of it, how the instrument would be lifted, secured, and placed in the van waiting just beyond the path.

"Walk?" he asked.

"Yeah. I don't want to go home yet."

They moved through the city without deciding on a destination out loud, their pace unforced, their direction shaped more by instinct than intention.

The streets carried more life than the park had—the sound of cars, distant voices, the occasional burst of music slipping through open windows reminding them that the world hadn't stopped. It had softened.

A passing car slowed at the light, bass rolling low from its speakers. Kia felt it immediately. *My mother used to play music like that.*

"The good days?" Ajah asked.

Kia nodded slowly. *"The really good ones."*

They turned a corner without discussing it, and as they continued walking, the sound reached her before the sight did—low, steady, alive.

Ajah noticed. *"You hear it."*

"I always do."

Washington Square Park opened before them, the arch standing wide and unmoved.

Beneath it, the energy was immediate—drums layered over voices, movement overlapping in ways that felt chaotic but held together.

Kia stopped at the edge.

Her breath stayed steady.

"You used to come here before you met me."

Kia let out a small breath. *"Yeah. This is where I learned I wasn't the problem."*

Ajah didn't respond right away. He let that truth stand.

She stepped forward—not into memory, but into recognition.

The drums met her. The voices moved around her.

"This place didn't fix me," she said quietly. *"It just let me feel everything without being punished for it."*

Ajah nodded. *"That's how you know it was real."*

Kia exhaled slowly.

And this time—she stayed.

Chapter Three: Where Sound Was Allowed to Breathe

The moment did not return to explain itself.

It moved.

The last note Ajah played settled behind them as they walked, no longer something to hold, but something that had already done its work.

The park shifted with them—the light thinning, shadows stretching, the city pressing gently back in—and Kia did not rush ahead of it or fall behind it. She walked inside it, present in a way that no longer required effort.

Ajah moved beside her, steady and unintrusive, his presence felt without needing to be named.

"You went somewhere back there."

Kia let out a quiet breath. *"I always do."*

They reached the edge of the park where the city began to rise again.

"You don't have to stay there."

Kia's mouth curved slightly, something thoughtful passing through her expression. *"I don't know how not to yet."*

Ajah nodded once. *"Then don't rush it."*

That was enough.

They stepped into the city, and the rhythm found her before she fully registered it—drums, low at first, then clearer, then undeniable.

She slowed.

Ajah noticed. *"You hear that."*

"Yeah."

They turned together, and Washington Square opened before them again—not as something new, but as something recognized differently.

Kia paused at the edge, her body responding out of memory before her mind caught up, her shoulders lifting slightly, her chest tightening in that familiar way.

Ajah stayed beside her.

"You want to go in?"

Kia didn't answer immediately. Her gaze moved across the space, taking in the movement, the openness, the absence of containment.

I used to come here.

"When?" Ajah asked.

Her throat tightened briefly—not from fear, but from memory. *"When I needed to feel something without getting in trouble for it."*

Ajah nodded. *"Then maybe you still do."*

She stepped forward.

The memory didn't pull her away. It met her where she stood.

A classroom. Heat rising. A sound leaving her before she could stop it. Silence rushing in behind it like it had been waiting.

At home, anger was not neutral. It started things. So she learned to hold it, to fold it, to carry it quietly.

Until she found this place.

Drums. Movement. Voices that didn't correct her.

A woman threw her head back and screamed—release, not fear—and the sound dissolved into everything around it.

Kia laughed.

Too loud. Too sudden.

Her hand moved instinctively toward her mouth. She waited.

Nothing came.

No correction. No consequence.

That stayed with her.

Kia.

She blinked. *"I'm here."*

Ajah nodded. *"I know."*

And he did.

Kia looked out again, her shoulders lowering, her breath evening as something settled into clarity.

She had not been drawn to chaos.

She had been drawn to space.

Space where she could feel—and remain whole.

The drums continued.

The night held.

And beside her—Ajah stayed.

Chapter Four: The Sound Between Them

The drums did not follow her when she stepped away from the center of the park, but their rhythm stayed—low, steady, no longer something she needed to release, but something her body carried without resistance.

As they moved farther from the arch, the sound softened into distance, folding into the layered noise of the city.

Traffic rolled low beyond the trees, voices passed in fragments, laughter rose and disappeared before it fully formed. The park stretched around them in long shadows and softened light, the hour settling into something quieter without losing its hold.

Kia walked beside Ajah without speaking, her pace slower now, more deliberate. She was aware of her movement—not as escape, but as presence—and for the first time, she didn't feel like she was adjusting ahead of herself.

She became aware of him differently.

Not as the steady presence she had come to rely on. Not as the quiet grounding she had learned to trust.

As a man.

It arrived without warning. Not as thought, but as recognition.

She noticed the way he walked first—deliberate without being rigid, unhurried without being passive. Each step placed with an ease that came from knowing where he stood, not just physically, but within himself.

There was no excess movement, no tension riding beneath the surface, no need to assert space or retreat from it. He moved like someone who understood both.

Her eyes shifted to his shoulders—broad, relaxed, carrying strength without display. Not rigid. Not guarded. Held.

Then his hands, now empty at his sides—but she remembered them differently. On the piano.

Controlled. Measured. Capable of restraint in ways that required more discipline than force.

Those hands had created space for her, had held her in sound, had guided her through something she had not known how to name—without ever touching her.

Her breath caught slightly.

Those same hands have been holding me…

The realization moved through her before she could shape it into anything more defined, settling just beneath her skin, unfamiliar not because it didn't belong, but because she had not allowed herself to stand inside it.

She looked away—not in rejection, but in regulation, her body adjusting before she gave it permission to stay.

Ajah noticed.

Of course he did.

He always noticed what moved before it was spoken.

But he didn't turn toward her immediately.

He didn't interrupt the moment by naming it. He let it exist, gave her space to decide what it meant—or if it meant anything at all.

"You're quieter than usual."

Kia exhaled softly, her gaze still forward.

"That's saying a lot?"

Ajah glanced at her, one eyebrow lifting slightly, his expression touched with quiet amusement. *"For you? Yeah."*

A small smile formed, but it didn't fully settle. Something else moved beneath it.

"I think I'm noticing things I didn't before."

Ajah didn't press. *"Like what?"*

The question stayed simple. Unloaded.

Kia hesitated—not because she lacked the answer, but because speaking it would give shape to something she had only just begun to feel. Her eyes dropped again to his hands, then lifted.

"Like how you don't rush anything."

Ajah's expression shifted slightly—awareness, not defense. *"That's not always a good thing."*

Kia shook her head, her voice quieter now, more certain. *"It is for me."*

That settled between them—not loud, not fragile, but anchored. The kind of truth that did not ask to be expanded, only acknowledged.

They reached a quieter stretch of the park where the sounds of the city softened into distance, and the space around them narrowed into something more contained.

A bench rested beneath a tree, its branches stretching outward, filtering the remaining light into a soft, diffused glow that wrapped the ground in warmth. The air felt different here—still, held.

They slowed without speaking, the decision mutual and unforced.

Ajah gestured lightly. *"You want to sit?"*

Kia nodded. *"Yeah."*

They sat with space between them—measured, intentional. Not distant. Not close.

Enough to feel each other's presence without assumption.

For a moment, nothing moved between them but breath.

Then Kia leaned forward slightly, her elbows resting on her knees, her hands loosely clasped as her gaze settled somewhere ahead of them, unfixed.

"Do you ever feel like you've been performing your whole life... and you don't know what's left when you stop?"

The question settled into the space—not heavy, but deep.

Ajah didn't answer immediately. He let it land, let it exist without rushing to respond.

"Yeah."

Simple. Unprotected. True.

Kia turned her head slightly, looking at him now, something in her expression softening with recognition. *"You?"*

Ajah's gaze drifted for a moment—not away from her, but through something that belonged to him. *"Music was the only place I didn't have to. Everywhere else... expectations come with you."*

Kia nodded slowly, her body understanding that before her mind needed to. *"Acting does that for me. It lets me feel everything—but sometimes I don't know how to turn it off."*

Ajah turned toward her then, more directly—not closing the space, but stepping into it.

"Maybe you're not supposed to turn it off. Maybe you're supposed to learn how to come back to yourself after."

That did not land as thought.

It landed as release.

Something in her chest tightened, then softened, like something long held in place had finally been given permission to move without consequence.

She looked at him fully now, and this time she did not filter what she felt through safety, or understanding, or control.

She felt him.

The space between them shifted—not dramatically, but undeniably. Like air changing before rain. Like something forming that did not need to be announced to be real.

And in that quiet—before either of them named it, before either of them reached for it, before either of them decided what it meant—something began.

Chapter Five: Where the Air Let Her Breathe

The feeling didn't leave her when the night ended. It stayed—quiet, steady, settled somewhere beneath everything she had just begun to understand, and without asking her permission, it carried her backward.

Not away from the present.

Into the place where she first learned the difference.

Tompkins Square Park did not announce itself. It did not rise to meet the city with spectacle or stretch outward to be admired. It existed the way certain things did when they had nothing to prove—settled, worn into place, shaped by time rather than design.

The Lower East Side moved around it. Buildings pressed close. Streets carried their usual weight—voices layered over traffic, footsteps overlapping without pause, life moving in directions that rarely asked permission. But inside the park, something shifted. Not silence. Not absence.

Something softer.

The benches held history in their wood, worn smooth in places where hands had rested too often to count, their surfaces carrying the quiet imprint of conversations that had long since ended but had never fully left.

The trees leaned slightly, their branches stretching outward in uneven directions, not reaching for perfection—just light. Leaves moved without urgency, brushing against one another in low, continuous motion, the sound subtle but constant.

It was not polished. Not controlled. It was honest.

And for Kia, honesty did not require anything from her. It did not turn on her. It did not change shape once she stepped inside it.

Her father brought her there without announcement—no explanation, no preparation, no moment where he named it as important. He simply reached for her hand one morning, the air still holding the cool edge of early day, and walked.

The streets unfolded beneath them in quiet transitions, from the tightness of their block where buildings leaned close and sound carried too easily between walls, to something more open. Sidewalks stretched just enough. Air moved differently. Noise didn't press.

Kia noticed before she understood.

Her shoulders lowered—not intentionally, her body releasing something it had been holding without asking permission first.

Her father didn't rush her forward when they reached the park. He slowed at the edge, let her stand there, let her see, let her decide how much of it she was ready to take in.

"You don't have to do nothing here," he said, his voice low and steady, the same tone he used when he wanted her to trust him without needing to question why. *"Just be."*

Kia didn't answer. She looked—not quickly, not passively.

She watched.

A man sat at a chess table, his fingers hovering above a piece, pausing in that space between decision and action. A woman walked two dogs who moved like the world beyond each other didn't exist, their steps matched in a quiet rhythm that didn't require direction.

A couple sat side by side on a bench, not speaking, but not distant—the space between them filled with something steady enough not to need conversation to hold it.

No one seemed to be bracing.

That difference didn't arrive all at once. It settled slowly, like warmth moving into a space that had been cold too long.

They chose a bench that didn't face anything specific. That mattered. Her father always chose spaces like that—places where she could see without being seen too closely, exist without becoming something for someone else to respond to.

He sat first, his presence grounding the space before she joined him, his body settling into the bench with ease, his hands resting loosely against his knees, his posture relaxed but aware.

Kia climbed up beside him. Her legs swung for a moment before she pulled them in, her body folding inward out of habit, her hands settling into her lap like they had learned to do without being told.

They sat.

No instruction. No expectation.

For a while, she watched everything—the movement, the stillness, the way people occupied space without explaining themselves.

It didn't match what she knew.

And because of that, she stayed careful—but not afraid.

"What you hear?" her father asked after a while, his voice soft enough not to interrupt what she had already begun doing.

Kia tilted her head slightly, her attention shifting.

She listened.

"Dogs," she said first.

He nodded. *"What else?"*

She softened her gaze, quieting what she could see.

"Talking," she said. *"But not loud."*

"Good," he said. *"Keep going."*

Kia inhaled slowly. Her breath caught slightly, then moved.

"Leaves," she said after a moment. *"They sound like... like paper."*

A small smile touched his face.

"That's right," he said. *"That's the wind talking through them."*

Kia looked up—really looked.

The trees weren't just standing.

They were moving.

Speaking.

"Why?" she asked.

He leaned back slightly, his gaze following hers.

"Because everything got a way it speaks. You just got to learn how to hear it."

That didn't become understanding right away.

It became something held.

They came back the next day. Then again.

Then again.

Not always at the same time. Not always for long. But often enough that the space stopped feeling unfamiliar.

It became known.

Her body learned it first—the way her breathing changed when she entered, the way the tightness in her chest didn't arrive as quickly, the way her shoulders didn't lift without reason.

Here, she did not have to stay ready.

Her father never filled the space with too much language. He let the park teach, let it hold what needed to be understood. But when he spoke, it mattered.

"When it get loud in your head," he said one afternoon, his gaze forward but aware of her, *"you don't fight it."*

Kia turned toward him slightly. *"Then what?"*

He tapped his fingers lightly against his knee—slow, rhythmic, grounded.

"You find something real. Something outside of it."

She frowned slightly—not disagreement, but searching.

He nodded toward the ground.

"Feel your feet. Right now."

Kia hesitated, then shifted her awareness downward. Her shoes pressed into the earth—solid, unmoving.

"It's not moving."

"Exactly," he said. *"So when everything else feel like it is—you remember that ain't."*

That stayed—not as instruction, but as return.

Some days, her mother came with them.

Those days carried a different rhythm—not wrong, not unsafe, different. Her mother moved slightly ahead, then behind, never quite settling into the same pace.

"Look, Kia," she would say softly. *"See how pretty that is."*

Kia would look.

And sometimes, she would see it—not through caution, but through her.

Those moments stayed longer than they should have—because they were real.

Her father never interrupted those moments.

But Kia noticed the way he watched.

Always watching.

Always present.

One afternoon, as the sun lowered and the park shifted again, Kia leaned into him—not consciously, not planned. Her shoulder brushed his arm, her body moving toward something it had already decided it trusted.

He didn't react.

He adjusted—slightly—making space.

Letting her stay.

"You like it here," he said after a while.

Not a question.

Kia nodded against him. *"It's quiet."*

He glanced down briefly.

"It ain't quiet."

She lifted her head, confused. *"It is."*

He shook his head gently.

"No. It's just not loud in the way that hurt you."

That difference didn't fully land then.

But it stayed.

Years later, standing in spaces filled with sound—drums, voices, music moving through bodies without restraint—Kia would not mistake it for danger.

Because she had learned, on worn benches beneath trees that spoke without words, beside a man who never rushed her understanding—
that not all noise was meant to break you.

Some of it—was meant to let you breathe.

Chapter Six: The Night She Didn't Have to Be Herself

What she learned in the park did not stay there.

It followed her—not as something she had to remember, not as instruction she needed to repeat to herself, but as a quiet shift that began to live inside her body before she could name it.

The understanding settled into her in pieces, showing up in moments she would not have expected, revealing itself not through silence, but through sound that did not demand she shrink from it.

And nowhere did that feeling return to her more fully than on Halloween.

Halloween did not arrive quietly in the East Village. It gathered—slow at first, almost unnoticed, then undeniable. Days before the night itself, the neighborhood began to change, the shift settling into storefronts, sidewalks, and the air itself, as if the city had made a quiet decision to loosen its hold on everything it usually kept in place.

Windows filled with masks—faces that did not hide but revealed something else entirely, exaggerated, distorted, playful, haunting, expressions that did not require explanation to be understood.

Fabric appeared where it did not belong. Glitter caught light in corners of shops that usually held nothing but necessity. Feathers, paint, color layered over brick and glass until the ordinary no longer felt fixed in the way it once had.

Music moved differently too. It no longer stayed inside. It spilled outward—rhythms rising from open doorways, drifting across sidewalks, blending into laughter that carried farther than usual, not contained, not corrected, simply allowed to exist as it was.

Kia felt it before she understood it.

The shift.

The permission.

Not spoken, not announced, but present in a way that did not ask her to question it.

Tonight, you don't have to be who you've been.

For a child who had already learned how to measure herself in every space she entered—how to adjust before she spoke, how to read the room before she moved inside it, how to remain within the edges of what felt safe—Halloween was not just a night of costumes and movement.

It was release.

Her father never made a show of what he did, but he prepared. He always prepared.

The costume was never something bought quickly and worn without thought. He built it.

His hands moved with the same precision he used in everything—steady, deliberate, patient in a way that made the process feel as important as the result.

Fabric was cut clean. Seams were reinforced. Details were added not for display, but for feeling—for the way the costume would sit on her body, for the way it would move with her rather than against her.

That year, she was a witch.

Not something exaggerated for attention.

Not something meant to frighten or entertain.

Something controlled.

The hat rested slightly off-center, not perfect but intentional. The dress fell around her in soft layers that shifted when she moved, catching light in a way that made her feel as though she existed just slightly outside of everything else she had known herself to be.

Kia stood in front of the mirror and turned slowly, not performing, not pretending—watching.

Watching the way the fabric followed her movement, the way her posture adjusted without her telling it to, the way her body occupied space differently.

Not smaller.

Not careful.

Allowed.

The smile that came did not pass through hesitation first. It did not check itself before settling. It stayed.

"You like it?"

Her father stood in the doorway, his arms resting loosely, his presence filling the space without pressing into it, his expression already holding the answer.

Kia turned toward him, her eyes brighter than usual, something unguarded moving through them. *"Yeah,"* she said, her voice lighter, freer. *"I don't feel like me."*

He nodded once, not correcting it, not softening it. *"That's the point."*

Her mother watched from the living room, her presence still but not distant. Her small frame held a quiet that could shift without warning, but tonight it did not. Her eyes moved across Kia, taking in every detail with a precision that missed nothing.

And on this night, she stayed present.

"She looks beautiful," she said, her voice soft, landing without sharpness.

Kia did not rush past the moment. She let it sit where it landed, let it remain what it was without questioning it. *"Thank you."*

Her mother smiled, and the smile held—long enough to be trusted.

"Stay close," she added gently. *"The streets will be full."*

Kia nodded, not out of fear, but understanding. When love came clearly, it was something you honored.

By the time they stepped outside, the streets were already alive—not yet overwhelmed, but building toward something that could not be held back.

People moved with intention, costumes brushing past each other in flashes of color and imagination, fabric shifting, masks catching light, identities loosening from what they were expected to be.

Kia held her father's hand at first, not tightly, not out of fear, but connection. The warmth of his hand grounded her, familiar, steady in a way that did not require her to check herself.

As they moved deeper into the Village, the energy rose around them. Sound layered over sound—music, voices, laughter, movement pressing into movement until the space itself felt alive in a way that could not be ignored.

And something inside her responded.

Her grip loosened—not fully, not all at once, but enough for the shift to be felt.

Her father felt it.

And he let it happen.

He always let her choose the moment.

The parade did not begin in a single instant.

It gathered, bodies pulling into place, movement forming before it was named, rhythm building before it was organized. And then it was there.

Drums moved through the street, not precise, not controlled, but alive, the sound rising through the pavement, traveling through her feet, into her body, settling somewhere deeper than hearing.

Costumes moved in waves—ghosts, dancers, creatures, kings—faces painted into expressions that did not ask to be understood, only to be seen as they were.

Kia stepped closer to the curb, her breath catching, not in fear, but in recognition of something she had not known she was allowed to feel.

People were loud.

Not reckless. Not out of control.

Unapologetic.

They laughed without covering their mouths. They moved without checking who was watching. They spoke, shouted, sang, their bodies existing fully in the space around them without waiting for permission.

And nothing happened.

No correction.

No interruption.

Nothing turned against them for being seen.

Something opened in her chest—not sharply, not painfully, but completely.

A group passed in a rush of glitter and color, their movement fluid and fearless, music following them, pulsing outward. The people around them did not step back—they joined, clapping, cheering, responding without hesitation.

Kia laughed.

The sound left her before she could stop it, bright, clear, unfiltered in a way she had never allowed it to be.

Her hand lifted halfway, instinct pulling it upward—then paused.

She waited for the shift.

It didn't come.

No one turned.

No one corrected.

No one asked her to pull it back.

Her hand lowered slowly, her breath unsteady, but not unsafe.

Beside her, her father watched—not the parade, not the crowd—her.

And when she looked at him, just for a moment, uncertain in a way that was new to her—he nodded.

"Go ahead."

Not permission.

Recognition.

Kia stepped forward—not fully into the street, not completely into the movement, but enough to feel it without losing herself inside it.

A performer moved close, their mask exaggerated, their body alive with motion, reaching toward her in a gesture that invited rather than demanded.

Kia hesitated only for a moment.

Then she mirrored it.

Small.

But real.

The performer laughed and spun away, dissolving back into the current without asking for anything more.

But the moment did not leave her.

Later, when the night softened and the crowd thinned just enough for movement to feel chosen instead of carried, Kia walked beside her father again.

Her body had changed—looser, lighter, not holding itself in the same way it had before.

She removed her hat slowly, holding it in her hands, her fingers tracing the edges as if trying to understand what it had allowed her to feel.

"Can I wear it again tomorrow?"

Her father glanced down at her, a small smile forming. *"Tomorrow ain't Halloween."*

She frowned slightly, not accepting that as the end of it. *"So?"*

A quiet chuckle moved through him. *"So tomorrow—you gotta be you again."*

Kia looked down at the hat, then back at the street, the movement, the people who were still lingering in pieces of what the night had allowed them to become.

Her thoughts moved differently now.

What if I like this me better.

The question stayed between them.

Her father did not rush to answer it.

He reached down instead, adjusting the hat gently back onto her head, his hands careful, intentional in the way they always were.

"Then you figure out what part of this belongs to you," he said. *"And you keep that."*

That stayed with her.

Not fully understood.

But felt in a way that did not need explanation.

And years later, standing in spaces filled with sound—drums, voices, movement that no longer required restraint—Kia would not mistake it for danger.

Because she had learned, not just in quiet places, but in moments where the world opened wide enough to hold everything without breaking—that sometimes the only way to understand who you are is to first experience who you are allowed to be when nothing asks you to become smaller.

Chapter Seven: Where the Streets Learned Her Rhythm

Summer did not arrive gently in the Lower East Side.

It pushed its way in, the same way everything else did when it refused to be ignored.

Windows opened not because anyone wanted fresh air, but because the heat insisted on entry.

Fire escapes held laundry, flowerpots, elbows, gossip.

Radios leaned into open sills, and music spilled outward without apology—salsa rolling into soul, gospel drifting into early hip-hop, bass lines threading beneath voices until the whole neighborhood sounded like competing truths learning how to live beside one another.

The sidewalks filled with bodies that refused to stay indoors, children running between legs and hydrants, old men in folding chairs fanning themselves with newspapers and opinions, women calling to one another from stoops, their voices rising above the traffic with a familiarity that made everything feel less separate than it was.

The city sweated, and in that sweat, it came alive.

Kia felt it before she understood it—the difference between noise that pressed against her and noise that pulled her in, the same distinction her body had begun to learn in quieter places, now returning to her in a space that did not lower itself to meet her, but expected her to meet it where it stood.

That was becoming one of the quiet recognitions of her childhood, the kind that didn't arrive in language first, but in the body.

Some sounds tightened her. Some sounds opened her. Some spaces made her smaller before she had even entered them.

Others widened around her, as if the air itself had decided she did not have to brace there—but here, the question was different now.

Not whether she was safe. Whether she belonged.

The Puerto Rican Day Parade did not begin with a start time she could feel. It began with anticipation.

Days before, the neighborhood shifted again, this time in color. Red, white, and blue flags with a single white star appeared in windows, draped across shoulders, tied around heads, waved from fire escapes as if they meant something larger than celebration.

Storefronts seemed brighter. Voices ran louder. The block looked less like a place people merely lived and more like a place people were preparing to claim.

Her father noticed her watching. He always noticed.

"You see that?" he asked, nodding toward a group gathered on the corner, their voices already louder than usual, their bodies moving with a charge she could feel before she could name.

She nodded. *"They happy."*

A small smile touched his face. *"More than that,"* he said. *"They proud."*

Kia turned the word over inside herself.

Proud did not feel like happy. Happy was quick. Happy could disappear. Proud felt heavier. Stronger.

Like it came with roots. Like it carried history she had not lived, but could still sense moving through the people around her.

The day of the parade, the streets no longer belonged to traffic. They belonged to people.

Music arrived first, moving through the pavement before it reached her ears—drums, horns, voices layered in a rhythm that felt coordinated without ever seeming controlled.

It rose from somewhere deeper than performance, something collective and bodily and alive.

Kia stood close to her father, not because she was afraid, but because the energy was bigger than anything she had stepped into before, and she needed something steady beside her while she learned how to read it.

Bodies moved in waves—not shoving, not colliding—flowing.

Women danced in ways that looked like language without words, their hips sure, their shoulders free, their arms lifting with a confidence that did not ask permission to take up space.

Men answered them, not overpowering, not dimming them, but matching, echoing, responding.

Children cut through everything like they had always belonged to joy in public.

Kia watched all of it, eyes wide, breath uneven, her body unsure whether it should stay still or move with what it was feeling.

A woman passed close, dress bright, earrings brighter, her laughter lifting ahead of her.

She said something in Spanish to someone behind her, the words fast and musical, her mouth shaping them with a confidence that made the language sound like movement itself.

Kia did not understand the words, but she understood the feeling—joy that did not apologize for arriving loudly.

"Why they dancing like that?" Kia asked, her voice low but urgent, as though she needed the

answer before the moment moved beyond her reach.

Her father didn't rush. He never rushed.

"Because they can," he said simply.

Kia frowned slightly. *"That's it?"*

He looked down at her, then back at the street. *"That's enough."*

The answer stayed with her, even without fully settling.

The music grew louder as the parade moved closer, shifting from something she could observe into something she could feel.

It reached her body the same way the drums had before—not asking permission, not waiting to see whether she was ready.

It moved through her anyway. Her fingers twitched first, then her shoulders, then her feet shifted lightly against the ground, almost before she knew she was doing it.

She stopped herself. That old instinct.

Pause. Check. Contain.

Her father noticed.

"You can move," he said quietly.

Kia looked up at him, uncertain. *"Right here?"*

He nodded once. *"Ain't nobody watching you the way you think they are."*

That was still hard for her to believe.

She let one foot move first, a small shift, then her shoulders, then her hands, not fully dancing, not confidently, but honestly.

The rhythm caught her. Across the street, a man saw her trying and grinned, lifting both hands in encouragement.

Not mocking. Not correcting. Just meeting her movement with recognition.

Kia hesitated, then smiled back. The moment passed without demand. And something inside her expanded.

The parade moved around her now, not something she had to chase, but something she could stand inside.

Flags waved overhead, flashing red, white, and blue against the summer light.

Voices rose and folded into one another, layered in languages she did not speak but did not feel excluded from either.

The whole street pulsed—not with disorder, but with presence.

She watched a woman throw her arms around another, their laughter unguarded, their joy public and unashamed.

She watched a group of men argue with heat and affection in the same breath, their hands moving sharply, their mouths quicker, but nothing in their energy suggesting rupture.

She watched children dance without rhythm, without instruction, without concern for how they looked.

And she felt it again—an opening in her chest, but clearer now, less like something she was stepping outside herself to access and more like something she could stand inside without disguise.

The shift inside her arrived before she could name it. A question began to form, small at first, then stronger.

Where do I belong in all of this?

She looked down at her hands, then at her skin, then back at the faces around her—brown, light, dark, varied in ways that did not ask to be simplified.

She felt connected and separate at the same time.

Her mother's features lived in her. Her father's presence lived in her. But here, in this street full of identity worn openly, joyfully, without apology, she did not know where she fit.

And for the first time, that did not frighten her. It stretched her.

"You thinking hard," her father said.

Kia looked up at him. *"I don't know what I am."*

Her father nodded once, slowly. *"You don't have to decide that today."*

Kia frowned. *"Then when?"*

He looked back at the street.

"When you stop asking it like it got one answer."

Then, softer: *"You ain't one thing... so don't try to fit yourself into one space."*

That stayed. Not fully understood. But enough.

The music swelled again. This time, when Kia stepped forward, she did not pause. She moved.

Her body found the rhythm more easily now—not polished, not practiced, but willing.

Her shoulders loosened.

Her hands followed.

Her steps adjusted without shame.

Her father watched. And for a moment—

Kia was not measuring herself.

Not adjusting. Not bracing. She was simply there.

Years later, when she would step onto a stage, slipping into characters that let her explore pieces of herself she had not yet named, she would carry this feeling with her—not the exact street, not the specific faces, not even the precise sound, but the truth of it.

Identity was not something handed to you once and for all.

It was something you moved through, something that expanded.

And sometimes belonging was not about choosing one place, but allowing yourself to exist fully in all the spaces that called something out of you.

Chapter Eight: The Girl Who Could Become Anyone

What she felt in the street did not leave her there.

It followed her—not as something she needed to name, not as something that settled into understanding, but as a presence that stayed with her as everything else began to change.

It did not arrive as clarity. It moved with her instead, stretching through her days, threading itself into moments that had nothing to do with the street and everything to do with what it had opened.

Adolescence did not arrive for Kia all at once. It came in layers.

A voice that no longer sounded entirely like a child's when it reached her own ears. A body that began changing without consultation, as if it belonged to time before it belonged to her.

Emotions that rose faster now—sharper, fuller, harder to name—and once they rose, harder to place back where they had come from.

But what unsettled her most was not the change itself. It was the intensity of it.

Everything felt louder. Not outside. Inside.

The apartment had not changed. Its walls still held the same sounds, the same pauses, the same emotional weather that could shift without warning and still somehow insist on being called ordinary.

Her mother still moved through moods that could not be predicted, her presence warm one moment and volatile the next, her voice capable of lifting a room or splintering it without any visible effort.

Her father still held the same steady rhythm, still rose early, still worked long hours, still came home carrying that quiet strength that never announced itself but always altered the air once he entered it.

But Kia had changed. And now she felt everything they felt, her body holding it longer than the room itself.

School became the first place where she noticed the difference clearly.

Not because school was warm.

Not because it was easy.

Because it was structured—predictable in ways her home life was not.

Classrooms had beginnings and endings.

Teachers followed plans written on boards.

Bells rang whether you were ready or not, signaling transitions that did not depend on anyone's mood, anyone's stability, anyone's capacity to hold the day together.

Desks stood where they had been left.

Hallways moved according to their own order. There was relief in that kind of architecture. Until there wasn't.

Because structure could hold a room. It could not hold what she carried into it.

Kia still brought herself with her—the awareness, the listening, the constant, silent scanning of tone and energy.

She noticed everything.

Who laughed too loudly and kept glancing around to see who noticed.

Who spoke too softly, as if they had learned early that attention cost more than it gave back.

Who wanted to be admired. Who wanted to disappear.

Which teachers smiled because they were kind and which smiled because they had learned how to keep order with performance.

She noticed who was trying to be seen. And who was trying not to be.

And somewhere between observing all of it and trying to exist inside it without being consumed by it—something in her began to shift.

It started small. A class assignment. A scene.

Nothing prestigious. Nothing that looked like destiny from the outside.

The teacher handed out scripts with the carelessness adults sometimes had around things they did not recognize as sacred.

Pages slid across desks, light and temporary, as if words only mattered once someone important said them.

To everyone else, they were paper, a task, a break from routine. Kia held hers differently.

Carefully. Like it already meant something.

"You'll read for the character on page three," the teacher said, her tone casual, unaware of what she had just placed in Kia's hands.

A character. Someone else. Someone with words already chosen. Feelings already written.

Reactions already allowed.

Allowed.

Kia looked down at the page, read the lines once, then again, then again. Not because she didn't understand them. Because she did. Too quickly.

The girl on the page was angry in a way Kia recognized without explanation.

Defensive in a way that felt familiar.

Tired of being spoken over.

Tired of being misunderstood.

Tired of swallowing what should have been said out loud.

By the time her turn came, something in her had already crossed over.

She stood. Her body felt different.

Not nervous. Not exactly.

But aware in a way that felt new and ancient at the same time, like a door had opened somewhere inside her and she had stepped toward it before deciding whether she should.

The classroom blurred slightly at the edges—not disappeared, receded.

She spoke. Not loudly. Not theatrically. Not with the kind of exaggerated emotion people mistook for talent.

She spoke honestly. And the words left her mouth as if they had been waiting. They landed in the room without resistance.

Her voice carried something the class had not expected—something lived, something immediate, something that made the air around the scene tighten and listen.

The girl on the page no longer felt imagined.

She felt present.

The room changed. Students who had been half-listening straightened without meaning to.

The teacher leaned forward slightly. Even the fluorescent lights seemed harsher for a second, making everything look more exposed.

And Kia felt something she had never felt before. Not attention. Not approval. Control.

She could feel something and it did not get her punished for it.

She could express something and it did not escalate into something she could not manage.

She could exist inside emotion and it stayed where it was supposed to stay.

Contained. Directed. Understood.

"Do that again," the teacher said, her voice sharper now, more focused, no longer casual.

Kia blinked. *"Again?"*

The teacher nodded. *"Exactly like that."*

Kia hesitated, because she didn't know if she could—not the same way.

The first time had not felt manufactured. It had felt found. And found things did not always come back on command.

But she tried. And when she did—it came again. Not identical. But true. The room responded again. And something inside her—something she had not known needed a place to live—settled.

After that, it did not stop.

She started noticing characters everywhere.

Not in a theatrical way. In an instinctive one. In books, yes. In films. In scenes. But mostly in people. A

woman on the train holding her purse too tightly while smiling too politely at everyone who passed.

A teacher whose clipped tone hid exhaustion just beneath professionalism.

A girl in class who kept flipping her hair and laughing two beats too late because she wanted to be chosen by a room that had not yet decided it needed her.

Kia began to understand that what she had been doing her whole life—watching, listening, adjusting—was not only survival. It was skill. And acting gave that skill shape.

At home, nothing had changed. And everything had. Her mother's voice still rose and fell without warning, her emotions still moving in directions that required vigilance more than understanding.

Her father still held the line, still grounded the space, still offered presence where no one else knew how. But now Kia had somewhere to put what she felt.

Or at least—somewhere to redirect it.

She practiced in her room, not formally, not with systems or methods or plans—just moments.

Standing in front of the mirror with the door closed and the air inside her room holding that faint mixed scent of lotion, paper, laundry, and summer dust warming on the sill.

Light from the window hit one side of her face harder than the other, splitting her reflection into shade and clarity.

She shifted her face. Her posture. Her voice.

Trying on expressions the way she had once tried on Halloween versions of herself.

Anger. Joy. Sadness. Confidence. Defiance. Calm.

She studied how they looked, then how they felt, then how long she could hold them before her own face tried to return.

At first, it stayed controlled. Intentional. She stepped into the emotion, then stepped out.

Clean. Contained. A door she could open. A door she could close.

But then—something changed.

One night, an argument filled the apartment and did not resolve.

It moved through the walls in waves, not loud enough to be chaos in anyone else's language, but loud enough for Kia's body to hear what was underneath it.

Her mother's voice sharpened, then dropped, then rose again, thinner this time.

Her father's stayed low, but that did not mean nothing was happening.

The whole apartment held itself too tightly.

Kia retreated to her room, not dramatically, automatically.

Her chest was full of something she could not release.

Her mind ran in circles without landing.

Her body felt tight in places that had no name.

She stood in front of the mirror.

And without planning to—she became someone else.

Not a character from a script. Not someone assigned. Someone necessary. Someone who could say what Kia could not say inside her own name.

Someone whose voice could hold force without consequence. Someone whose anger did not have to disappear before it was heard.

Her posture shifted. Her chin lifted. Her eyes hardened. Her voice changed.

And the words came.

Not rehearsed. Not written. But real.

"You don't get to do that," she said, her reflection staring back at her with a strength she did not recognize. *"You don't get to make everything feel like it's about to fall apart."*

Her heart pounded so hard she could feel it in her throat. Her breath came fast.

But she didn't stop.

She kept going. Letting it out. Letting the invented self carry what her own body could no longer hold politely. Hold it. Contain it. Translate it.

And when it was over—she did not step out.

Not right away.

She stood there. Still inside it. Still feeling the shape of that other self around her like clothing she had not realized fit.

That was the first time.

After that, it happened more often. Not intentionally. Not planned. She would step into something—and stay there. Longer than she meant to. Longer than felt comfortable. But also—longer than she wanted to leave.

Because inside the character, things made sense. Emotion had direction. Reaction had structure. Pain belonged somewhere specific.

Nothing spiraled without purpose.

At school, her performances improved.

Teachers noticed. Students noticed. She became someone people watched—not because she tried to be watched, but because she held attention the same way she held silence.

Effortlessly. Unintentionally. Completely.

"You're different when you do that," a classmate said one afternoon, their tone curious, not critical.

Kia tilted her head. *"Different how?"*

The classmate shrugged. *"Like you mean it more than everybody else."*

Kia didn't answer. Because she didn't know how to explain that she did. She always had.

At home, her father noticed the change too—not the applause, not the school recognition, the stillness after.

The way she carried herself when she wasn't speaking. The way her eyes held onto something that did not always match the moment she was standing in. The way she seemed to return from somewhere, but not all the way.

One night he stood in her doorway longer than usual, watching, not interrupting, just seeing.

"You alright?" he asked finally.

Kia nodded too quickly. *"Yeah."*

He stepped inside. Sat beside her the same way he always had. No announcement. No shift in tone to make the moment larger than it needed to be. Just presence.

"You don't have to carry everything the way you do," he said quietly.

Kia looked down at her hands. *"I'm not."*

But her voice didn't match the words.

Her father didn't argue. Didn't correct. He simply placed his hand over hers, grounding, steady, real.

"Just make sure you know which parts of you are yours," he said.

Kia swallowed.

Because she wasn't sure anymore.

Years later, standing in front of a stage, slipping into roles that fit her like second skin, receiving applause that told her she had done it right—she would still feel it.

That line.

Thin.

Blurring.

The space between who she was—and who she could become.

And sometimes—when the lights dimmed and the room returned to itself—she wouldn't know which one had come back.

Chapter Nine: Applause That Didn't Follow Her Home

What she saw in the mirror did not settle.

It stayed with her—not loudly, not in a way that demanded attention, but in the quiet spaces between moments, where nothing performed and nothing explained itself.

The absence of a role did not bring clarity. It left something open beneath everything she did, everything she said, everything she allowed herself to feel without structure.

High school did not ask Kia who she was. It told her who she could be.

The building carried that kind of authority, announcing itself every morning in noise before thought had fully settled—lockers slamming like punctuation marks, sneakers squeaking against polished hallways, teachers calling out names with the practiced urgency of people trying to keep order from breaking into personality.

Everything moved fast. Everything reflected something. The walls held posters about excellence, performance, achievement, belonging, as if identity were something that could be assigned by hallway, period, and extracurricular commitment.

The place thrummed with expectation. And expectation, Kia was learning, had its own sound.

Voices rose and dropped depending on who had entered the room. Laughter changed shape depending on who was listening. Girls adjusted themselves in mirrors they pretended not to need.

Boys performed confidence with the loose carelessness of people who had not yet learned how visible insecurity could be.

Even stillness felt deliberate there.

Everything looked like a stage—whether anyone admitted it or not, people trying on versions of themselves the way they tried on clothes, some too big, some too tight, some worn long after they had stopped fitting just because they had once drawn the right kind of attention.

Kia understood that instinctively. She had been doing it long before anyone had a name for it. But now—it had direction.

The first time she stepped onto the high school stage, it wasn't new. Not entirely. But it was different. Bigger. Brighter. Less forgiving.

The stage smelled like dust warmed by light, old curtains, paint, wood that had been stepped on by years of students trying to become something unforgettable for two hours before returning to classrooms that barely remembered what they had just done.

The wings held nervous energy in pockets—half-whispered lines, dry mouths, shifting feet, costume fabric brushing against itself in restless friction.

Kia stood in the shadows before her entrance, still. Her hands quiet at her sides, her breathing controlled, her body held in a way that looked calm to anyone watching from the outside. But it wasn't calm. It was focus.

It was preparation. It was the careful alignment of everything inside her so that when she stepped out—nothing would spill where it didn't belong.

The lights beyond the wings did not warm the stage.

They exposed it.

The audience did not disappear into darkness the way movies made it seem.

They waited. Present. Expectant. Ready to receive or reject whatever she offered them.

"You ready?" someone whispered behind her.

Kia didn't turn. Didn't let the question break the line she had already crossed inside herself.

"Yeah."

And when her cue came—she moved.

The character met her immediately. Not something she had to search for, not something she reached toward, something she stepped into as naturally as breath once it had found the right rhythm.

Her posture shifted. Her voice changed. Her eyes sharpened into something clearer than the uncertainty she carried through hallways and home.

The words came not as memorization but as arrival, as if they had always belonged somewhere inside her and had only been waiting for the right frame to emerge without consequence.

She felt them move through her body with precision—shoulders, jaw, breath, timing—everything aligning without resistance.

Everything else fell away—the audience, the lights, the distance between her and the edge of the stage, the students in the wings, the room itself.

For those moments she was not adjusting, not measuring, not bracing.

She was exact.

That feeling landed in her harder than applause ever could.

To feel something fully and have it fit where it was meant to go—without correction, without escalation, without anything spilling beyond what she could hold.

Just form. Just direction. Just truth with somewhere to stand.

The applause came fast. Loud. Immediate.

It rushed toward her in a single wave, hands striking together from all directions, the room giving back what she had given it with a certainty that felt almost physical.

She stood there a second longer than necessary, her chest rising, pulse steadying, letting the sound hit her without shrinking from it.

It told her she had done something right.

Something complete. Something that landed exactly where it was supposed to.

Then she stepped back.

And just like that—it was gone.

Backstage did not hold the same clarity. It never did.

Voices overlapped.

People moved too quickly.

Costumes shifted.

Someone laughed too hard.

Someone cursed because they missed a cue.

Somebody was always looking for a hairpin, a line, a shoe, a place to put what they were feeling before the next scene began.

The energy changed shape instantly—performance folding into release, focus dissolving into noise.

But this chaos felt different. Lighter.

Unattached. Temporary. It did not threaten to become anything larger than itself. It didn't linger with teeth.

"That was amazing," someone said, grabbing her arm briefly before moving on.

Kia nodded. *"Thank you."*

The words came easily. Automatically.

But the feeling did not stay.

The precision vanished faster than it arrived.

The applause lingered in her ears for a little while, but not in her body. Whatever exactness she had found on the stage seemed to belong to the stage itself, dissolving the moment she stepped off it.

In the hallway the next day, people looked at her differently. Not dramatically, not in a way that changed the architecture of her life, but enough.

Enough to notice. Enough to understand that something had happened in a room and followed her into brighter spaces.

"You killed that," a boy said as he passed her, his tone casual, sincere.

Kia smiled. *"Thanks."*

He slowed slightly, matching her pace. *"You always like that?"*

She tilted her head. *"Like what?"*

He shrugged. *"Like… you disappear and then come back as somebody else."*

Kia laughed.

But it didn't fully land.

"I don't disappear."

She wasn't sure that was true.

His name was Marcus.

Not loud. Not trying too hard. The kind of presence that did not force itself into a room but did not vanish into one either.

He carried himself with a quiet steadiness that made him easy to miss if you were only watching for spectacle—but hard to forget once you actually noticed him.

He walked with her sometimes after school.

Not every day. Not predictably enough to become routine. But often enough that his company began to feel familiar. Comfortable.

They talked. About school. About music.

About teachers they liked and teachers they performed liking. About things that did not require too much from either of them.

And that—felt safe.

One afternoon they sat on the steps outside the school, the day stretched open in front of them, sunlight landing just right across the brick, the railings warm from hours of heat.

Around them, students passed in bursts—voices, backpacks, movement—everyone headed somewhere, even if only toward a bus stop or corner store.

Marcus looked at her longer than usual. Not invasive. Not searching. Curious.

"You ever get tired of it?"

Kia frowned slightly. *"Of what?"*

He leaned back on his hands, eyes turned toward the street. *"Being who everybody need you to be."*

That question landed differently. Not sharp.

Not accusatory. But direct in a way she had not prepared for.

Kia looked down at her hands, her fingers tracing the edge of her sleeve without thinking.

"I don't do that."

Marcus didn't argue. Didn't push. Didn't smile like he knew better.

He just nodded once.

"Alright."

The conversation moved on.

But the question didn't.

It stayed with her. Followed her home. Sat in the room with her when nobody else did.

Because what unsettled her was not that he had asked it. It was that some part of her had recognized it before she could reject it.

At home, nothing had changed. And everything had.

Her mother's presence still shifted without warning.

Her father still held steady. But Kia was harder to read now—even to herself.

She spent more time in her room. Not hiding. Not exactly.

But existing in a space where she could move between versions of herself without interruption.

Her room carried its own atmosphere now—the mirror, the bed, scattered papers, the faint scent of lotion and dust and stage makeup she had started experimenting with in careful amounts.

The mirror always stayed where it was.

Waiting.

The mirror became both tool and trap.

She stood in front of it longer now, her expressions more precise, her transitions smoother, her ability to shift from one emotion to another becoming something she could do without thought.

That should have felt like control.

Sometimes it did.

But not always.

Sometimes—it felt like distance.

One night, after rehearsal, she came home later than usual, her body still carrying the after-current of the character she had just played.

Her voice had not fully settled back into itself. Her walk still held some of the posture, some of the weight, some of the emotional angle of someone who was not quite Kia and not entirely gone.

Her father was in the living room.

Waiting.

Not impatient. Not questioning. Just present.

"You eat?"

Kia shook her head. *"Not yet."*

He nodded toward the kitchen. *"There's food on the stove."*

She moved toward it slowly.

He watched her.

"You still in it."

Kia paused.

Her back still turned.

"In what?"

He leaned forward slightly.

"That role," he said. *"You ain't put it down yet."*

Kia exhaled. *"It takes a minute."*

He nodded. *"I know."*

Then, after a pause: *"Just don't let it take more than it give back."*

She didn't answer.

Because she didn't know if she could.

Later that night, standing in front of the mirror again, Kia stared at herself longer than usual.

Her face.

Her eyes.

Her posture.

She shifted slightly.

Softened her expression.

Then hardened it.

Then let it go completely.

For one moment—nothing held. No role. No scene. No borrowed emotional frame. Just her.

And it felt unclear.

Unfinished.

I don't know where I am in myself.

Her chest tightened.

Not sharply.

But enough.

She inhaled slowly, breath catching halfway, her mind reaching for something to settle into—a voice, a posture, a role, something that would return shape to her body.

Nothing came immediately.

And for the first time—that frightened her.

Years later, when applause would come louder, longer, more sustained than anything she had experienced in those early school performances, she would understand something she could not yet fully grasp: Applause confirmed what you gave.

But it did not tell you who you were when the performance ended.

And if you didn't know that already—you could lose yourself trying to find it in the sound.

Chapter Ten: The Night She Didn't Come Back Right Away

What applause left behind did not disappear.

It lingered—not in sound, not in recognition, but in the quiet absence that followed it, in the space where something had been confirmed but nothing had been answered.

The stage had given her something exact, something complete, but when it was over, that clarity did not come with her.

What remained instead was something less defined, something that moved beneath her awareness without settling, without form.

The role did not end when the curtain closed. That was the first time it stayed with her long enough to matter.

It had been a heavier part than the others—less about words than what lived underneath them, a girl who held too much, a girl who spoke too late, a girl who had learned how to swallow emotion until it came out sharp and misplaced, landing on whoever stood closest when it finally broke free.

Kia had understood her immediately, too immediately, and that should have been the warning.

Backstage, the energy surged the way it always did after a strong performance. Voices overlapped, bodies moved too quickly, laughter spilled out in bright, uneven bursts that tried to shake off whatever had just been carried onstage.

Costume pieces changed hands, water bottles rolled beneath folding chairs, someone cursed because they'd missed a cue, someone else kept repeating a line as if afraid it might leave their body if they stopped saying it.

The room was full of release, but Kia stood in the middle of it still, the character not releasing her yet, sitting in her chest, in her throat, in the way her body held itself too tightly for the moment she was in.

Her hands remained slightly curled as if they were still holding emotion that no longer had lines attached to it, her shoulders stayed drawn in, even her breathing belonged to the girl she had just played—measured, compressed, carrying more than it let through.

"Kia, that was insane," someone said, brushing past her, their voice bright, celebratory, already moving on before the words could fully land.

She nodded. *"Thank you."* The words came out right. The tone didn't.

Marcus found her near the edge of the stage where the shadows from the wings still held a little quiet.

His presence cut through the noise without adding to it, and that was what she liked about him—he never seemed interested in filling space just because it was there. He studied her for a second longer than usual, his brow tightening just slightly.

"You good?"

Kia turned toward him, her eyes landing on his face but not quite settling there. *"Yeah."* But the voice that answered him carried something else, something distant, something not fully hers.

Marcus didn't move, didn't accept it.

"Nah," he said quietly. *"You still in it."*

The words landed harder than they should have. Kia felt her chest tighten around them, not because they were wrong, but because they were too close to something she had not yet named. *"It'll pass,"* she said.

Marcus nodded, but his expression didn't ease. *"Just don't stay there too long."*

The same warning. Different voice. Same concern.

The walk home felt longer than usual, not because the distance had changed, but because her awareness had.

Every sound reached her sharper than it should have—the scrape of a gate, a car turning too fast, someone laughing half a block away.

Every movement felt slightly delayed, as if the world were arriving a second after she saw it instead of all at once.

People passed her without becoming fully real, she heard voices without processing words, streetlights blurred softly at their edges.

The city moved as it always did, but she felt misaligned inside it, as if her body had kept walking while some essential part of her remained behind under the stage lights. Her feet kept moving, but part of her stayed.

By the time she reached home, the role had not loosened. If anything, the walk had sealed it in place.

When she stepped into the apartment, the shift hit her immediately—not loud, not explosive, but present. The kitchen light was on, too bright, casting a hard yellow across the floor and sharpening every edge in the room.

Her mother stood near the counter, her small frame rigid, her movements clipped in a way that signaled something had begun before Kia ever turned the doorknob.

A dish sat too close to the edge of the sink, a cabinet door wasn't fully closed, and the air held the kind of tension that made ordinary objects look like evidence.

Her father sat at the table, still, his posture grounded but alert, like he had been holding the room in place long enough for it not to fall apart while waiting to see what would happen next.

Kia paused in the doorway, her senses sharpening. The character inside her recognized this space too well.

"You're late," her mother said without turning. The words were simple. The tone wasn't.

Kia stepped inside slowly, her bag still over her shoulder, her body not fully adjusting to the room she had entered. *"Rehearsal ran over."*

Her voice carried the residue of the role—measured, contained, holding more than it revealed, and even to her own ears it sounded wrong for this room.

Her mother turned then, her eyes landing on Kia with a sharpness that cut through whatever distance the walk home had left in her. *"You always have a reason."*

Something rose in Kia's chest, not new, but faster than usual, stronger. The character heard the accusation before Kia did and responded first. *"Because there is one."*

Her father's head lifted slightly. That wasn't her usual tone. The room shifted—not visibly, but enough.

Her mother's expression changed, her energy rising, voice climbing just slightly higher, faster, sharper. *"Don't talk to me like that."*

Kia's hands tightened at her sides, her breath shortened, heat rose behind her face, everything in her narrowing into one clean, precise line. The character leaned forward. *"Like what?"*

The words came out too clean, too exact, carrying no softness, no uncertainty, no child.

Her father stood, not abruptly, but intentionally. *"Kia."* His voice came low, grounding, calling her back into the room she was actually standing in, but she didn't come—not right away—because the role had not released her.

Her mother stepped closer, her presence filling the space in a way that demanded answer, demanded reaction, demanded escalation.

Her emotions moved in that old familiar rhythm—rising, shifting, sharpening too fast to predict and too fast to stop once they had begun.

"You think you grown now?" she said, voice tight. *"You think you can say whatever you want?"*

Kia felt the heat rise higher, her chest tightening, her thoughts narrowing into something honed and dangerous.

The girl she had just played stood up inside her fully. *"I think I can answer you."*

Her father moved between them then, not blocking, not shoving, placing himself in the space where the moment had begun to take shape. *"That's enough."*

But by then, the shift had already happened.

Kia stepped back suddenly, her breath catching, her body reacting to something she hadn't fully understood until it was fully underway.

Chapter Eleven: The First Time Her Breath Belonged to Her

She did not return to herself all at once.

What happened that night did not disappear when the room went quiet, did not resolve just because the moment had passed.

It stayed with her in ways she could not immediately name—subtle at first, then clearer, then something she could no longer ignore.

The awareness that something inside her could move without her permission, could take shape before she could stop it, did not leave her untouched.

It followed her forward.

Time moved.

Not in a way that erased what happened—but in a way that gave it distance.

And with that distance—came space.

College did not feel like escape. It felt like space—not the kind that removes you from what shaped you, but the kind that finally lets you turn and look at it without being swallowed whole.

Kia noticed it the first morning she woke up in her dorm room, sunlight stretching across unfamiliar walls, soft at the edges, settling into corners that held no memory of raised voices, no imprint of tension waiting to be triggered.

The ceiling above her was plain, still, unmarked by anything but light, and the air felt different—lighter, but not empty, neutral in a way she had never experienced long enough to trust.

There were sounds, of course—doors opening down the hall, footsteps moving past at different paces, laughter breaking unevenly into the quiet, rising and falling without warning—but none of it pressed against her, none of it carried weight, none of it asked her to prepare.

For the first time in her life, the noise around her was not a warning.

She lay there longer than necessary, not because she didn't want to get up, but because she didn't have to rush the moment.

Her hands rested on her stomach, fingers loosely folded, her breathing slow, steady, unforced. No one was arguing in the next room, no voices were shifting unpredictably between warmth and storm, no part of her needed to anticipate what might happen next before she even moved.

She inhaled deeply and waited, and nothing followed it—no tightening, no correction, no sudden emotional shift she had to respond to. Just breath. It entered, it stayed, it left, uninterrupted, and for a moment that alone felt unfamiliar enough to matter.

Classes gave her language, not immediately, not all at once, but gradually, in ways that felt like pieces of something she had always known finding their place in a structure that finally held them without distortion.

Words appeared first as vocabulary—environment, conditioning, emotional regulation, trauma response—and at first they sounded clinical, distant, like something that belonged to textbooks and studies and other people's lives.

But as the weeks passed, those words began to align with her lived experience in ways that made her sit up a little straighter, listen a little closer, stay a little longer after class without realizing it, because what they described she had already felt; they just gave it shape.

She didn't speak much at first. She listened.

Watched how other people told their stories.

Some spoke easily, their emotions moving freely between words. Some hesitated, editing themselves in real time. Some detached completely, describing things that should have carried weight as if they were recalling something that had happened to someone else.

Kia recognized all of it—not intellectually, but in her body—but what stayed with her most was not what people said; it was what they allowed themselves to feel without apology.

One afternoon, seated in a lecture hall that smelled faintly of old wood, paper, and the quiet accumulation of years, Kia found herself writing something she hadn't planned.

The professor's voice moved steadily at the front of the room, grounded, measured, explaining systems and responses and patterns that could be observed, studied, named, but Kia had already drifted inward.

Her pen moved across the margin of her notebook—not notes, not definitions, just a sentence: *It wasn't me.* She stared at it, the ink still fresh, her pen hovering just above the page as if unsure whether to continue or stop there.

Her chest tightened slightly, not panic, not fear, something quieter—recognition. The words did not feel like an excuse; they felt like a separation, a line, something she had not known she needed to draw until it appeared.

The professor continued speaking, but Kia was somewhere else—not backward, not lost in memory, but inward.

Later that day, she walked without direction, campus giving way to city the way it always did—seamless, layered, alive. The transition didn't require effort; it didn't ask her to choose where one ended and the other began.

It simply shifted around her as she moved, buildings widening, sidewalks stretching, traffic thickening, people folding into one another in patterns that felt familiar without feeling invasive.

She walked slower than she usually did, her body no longer bracing for impact that wasn't coming, her shoulders dropping, her steps softening, and she didn't realize where she was going until the air changed, until the sound thinned, until the movement around her opened instead of pressed. Trees. Light filtering differently. Space.

Central Park.

It felt different now, not because it had changed, but because she had. The openness didn't overwhelm her, the space didn't feel like something she needed to cross quickly or justify being in; it simply existed, and for the first time she allowed herself to exist inside it without performing.

She found a bench without thinking and sat, her hands resting loosely in her lap, fingers no longer curled around tension she had learned to carry automatically.

Her gaze moved without urgency—people walking, dogs pulling gently at leashes, sunlight catching on leaves that shifted just enough to make the light feel alive—and her body softened, not dramatically, not all at once, but enough.

The music reached her before she saw him—not loud, not calling for attention, but present in a way that made everything else step slightly to the side.

A piano—clean, measured, each note placed with intention but without strain, without urgency, without performance.

Kia turned her head slowly, her attention following the sound until she saw him, positioned just far enough from the main path that the music felt discovered, not presented. Ajah.

He was younger than she expected someone with that kind of command over sound to be, but there was nothing uncertain about the way he played.

His posture was relaxed, shoulders loose, hands moving across the keys with a familiarity that did not look practiced—it looked lived.

The piano sat mounted on a wheeled frame, placed with care, angled just enough to catch light without reflecting it harshly, belonging there in a way that didn't interrupt the space.

He didn't look up when she approached, didn't acknowledge her in any visible way, but something in the music shifted slightly, subtly, as if the space had adjusted to include her.

Kia stood there for a moment, her body recognizing something before her mind did. The same stillness she had felt in her dorm room returned, but this time it carried warmth—not absence, but presence.

She sat on the nearest bench, unhurried, her attention settling fully into the way the music moved, not filling the air, not overtaking it, but shaping it.

He played like he trusted silence, like he understood it, like he didn't need to prove anything to it.

"You always listen this closely?" His voice came without breaking the music, low, even, threaded between notes in a way that felt placed rather than inserted.

Kia blinked slightly, caught not by the question, but by the fact that he had noticed her without needing to look. *"I think so."*

He nodded, still playing. *"Most people don't. They hear. They don't listen."*

Kia's eyes followed his hands, the movement, the restraint. *"What's the difference?"*

This time, he glanced at her—brief, but complete, not scanning, not assessing, seeing.

Listening means you let it change something." Then his attention returned to the keys.

Kia felt that, not as an idea, but as truth, because something inside her had already shifted, and she hadn't tried to stop it.

They didn't speak much after that, not that day. She stayed until the music ended, her body settled in a way she could not remember experiencing without effort—not managed, not controlled, just settled.

When he finally lifted his hands from the keys, the silence that followed didn't feel empty; it felt complete.

"You play here every day?"

He adjusted something near the edge of the piano, precise, unhurried. *"Most days. When the weather lets me."*

She nodded. *"Why here?"*

He looked out across the park before answering, taking in the space the same way he moved through music. *"Because people don't come here to hide. They come here to be."*

Kia exhaled softly. That landed more than she expected.

"I'm Kia."

He looked at her again, this time longer, still not invasive, still not searching, intentional.

Ajah."

The name settled between them, no explanation needed.

She didn't stay much longer, not because she wanted to leave, but because something told her not to rush what had just happened.

She stood, her body lighter than when she arrived, her breath still steady, her thoughts quieter—not empty, not resolved, but organized.

As she walked away, she noticed something she hadn't felt in a long time—not safety, she knew that, not control, she had learned that, but something else, something softer, less guarded, less prepared.

She felt seen—without performance, without effort, without needing to become anything other than what she already was.

Years later, she would understand that moment differently, not as a beginning that announced itself, not as something sudden, but as recognition—of something steady, something that would not demand, would not rush, would not overwhelm, but would remain. And for someone who had spent her entire life learning how to survive chaos, that kind of presence felt like love before she was ready to call it that.

Chapter Twelve: The Language for What Lived Inside Her

The second semester didn't arrive loudly. It unfolded, like something that had been waiting—not for the calendar, but for her.

Kia no longer moved through campus like a visitor studying the environment; she moved like someone who had begun to belong to herself within it.

Her steps slowed, not from hesitation but from choice, her shoulders lowering, no longer braced for interruption that hadn't yet occurred.

Her eyes didn't scan for disruption the way they once had, didn't search every room for the first sign of something shifting out of place.

There was still awareness, still sensitivity, still that quiet attunement to tone and energy and change, but it no longer controlled her movements—it informed them. That difference changed everything.

She spoke more in class now, not often, but intentionally, and when she did, her words didn't rush ahead of her thoughts.

They didn't spill out trying to get there first or soften themselves before they landed.

They arrived—measured, deliberate, carrying both experience and something new: understanding.

One afternoon, the conversation drifted toward family dynamics, emotional development, the ways environments shape behavior long before language is available to explain it.

Students spoke in turns—some careful, some detached, some rehearsed in ways that felt practiced rather than present.

Kia listened, as she always had, but something rose in her chest, not sharp, not overwhelming, just present enough that ignoring it would have felt like stepping away from herself.

She raised her hand, and the room shifted subtly but enough—heads turning, the professor's gaze settling, the space adjusting to hold what might be said.

Kia felt it and didn't retreat from it. *"Sometimes,"* she began, her voice steady but careful, *"you don't realize something wasn't normal until you're somewhere that doesn't feel like survival."*

The words didn't rush; they landed.

The professor nodded once, encouraging, not interrupting.

Kia continued, her eyes focused forward but her awareness stretched wider, holding both the room and something older at the same time. *"And then it's not just about understanding what happened,"* she said. *"It's about figuring out who you are without it."*

Silence followed—not empty, not uncomfortable, but held, the kind of silence that doesn't collapse under weight but receives it.

The professor leaned slightly forward. *"And what does that feel like?"*

Kia exhaled softly, her chest shifting, something loosening. *"Like learning how to breathe again,"* she said, *"but not trusting it at first."*

She didn't realize how much that moment had taken from her until she stepped outside. The air felt sharper against her skin, not cold but clear, her body heavier, not overwhelmed but open, and openness, she was learning, came with its own kind of vulnerability.

It wasn't the chaos she had grown up navigating; it was something quieter, something that asked her to stay present without defense.

She walked without deciding to, her body already choosing direction before her thoughts caught up.

Campus gave way to city the way it always did—without ceremony, without transition markers, just a gradual shift in density, in sound, in pace—and then the air changed, the sound thinned, the space widened.

Central Park met her again, not because it had changed, but because she had. The openness no longer felt like something she had to cross or justify; it didn't ask her to move faster, didn't ask her to fill it.

It simply existed, and this time she allowed herself to exist inside it without question. She found a bench without searching and sat, her hands resting loosely in her lap, fingers no longer curled around anticipation, her gaze moving slowly—people walking, dogs darting forward then circling back, sunlight breaking through branches that shifted just enough to make the light feel alive—and her body softened, not dramatically, but enough.

The music was already there, not approaching, not building, but present—a piano, measured, unrushed, each note placed with intention but without weight, without demand, without needing to prove itself.

Kia turned her head; she didn't have to look far. Ajah.

He didn't look surprised when she approached—he rarely did—but the music shifted slightly, not enough for anyone else to notice, enough for her.

She sat closer this time, not beside him, not distant, but between, a space that didn't require explanation.

He let the piece finish. That was something she had come to understand about him—he didn't interrupt what needed to complete itself. When his hands lifted from the keys, the silence that followed stretched, not empty, not unfinished, but intentional.

"You sound different today."

Kia blinked slightly. *"Different how?"*

He turned his head just enough to look at her, present, not searching. *"Less guarded,"* he said, *"but more aware of it."*

She let out a small breath, something between a laugh and release. *"That sounds complicated."*

He nodded once. *"It usually is."*

She looked down at her hands, still holding something from earlier. *"I said something in class today."*

He didn't respond immediately. He waited.

"Not unusual," he said after a moment.

"You talk."

She shook her head slightly, a faint smile forming. *"Not like that."*

He leaned back slightly, giving space, not distance. *"What'd you say?"*

Kia hesitated, not because she didn't want to share, but because saying it again would make it real in a different way, but something about him made that feel possible. *"I said that you don't always know something wasn't normal until you're somewhere that doesn't feel like survival."*

The words settled between them.

Ajah didn't reshape them, didn't soften them, didn't reach to interpret them. He let them remain intact. *"That's true."*

Kia looked at him, something in her chest loosening—no correction, no analysis, just acknowledgment.

"I think I'm still figuring out what that means for me."

Ajah nodded. *"You will,"* he said. *"You already started."*

She frowned slightly. *"How do you know?"*

He glanced toward the piano, then back.

"Because you can say it out loud now," he said. *"That's where it begins."*

Kia leaned back, her gaze lifting toward the sky breaking through branches in fragments.

"It's strange," she said. *"Understanding something doesn't automatically change how it feels."*

Ajah smiled slightly. *"It's not supposed to,"* he said. *"Understanding gives you direction. Feeling takes its time."*

She let that settle, because it didn't fix anything, but it felt right.

The quiet between them held. It always did—not empty, not waiting, just present.

After a while, she spoke again, more softly.

"Sometimes I don't know who I am without reacting to something." The words came slower, heavier, more exposed.

He didn't move.

"Like if nothing's happening," she continued, *"I don't know what I'm supposed to feel. Or how I'm supposed to be."*

The vulnerability in it wasn't loud, but it was real.

Ajah rested his hands on his knees, relaxed, present. *"You're not supposed to be anything."*

Kia looked at him. *"That doesn't make sense."*

He nodded. *"It doesn't at first,"* he said.

"But it's real." Then, after a brief pause, *"You've been responding your whole life. That's not the same as being."*

The distinction landed deep, because it separated something she had never been able to name.

"So how do you just... be?"

Ajah exhaled softly, his gaze drifting outward. *"You start small,"* he said. *"You sit. You breathe. You notice what doesn't hurt. You let that count."*

Kia swallowed, her throat tightening slightly. *"That feels too simple."*

He smiled faintly. *"Simple doesn't mean easy."*

The wind moved through the trees, light shifting, sound carrying softly from the edges of the city.

Kia closed her eyes, not long, just enough—her breath, the bench, the ground, the space, him—

and when she opened her eyes, something had softened, not resolved, not finished, but less tight.

"Can I ask you something?"

Ajah nodded. *"You just did."*

She smiled. *"You always like this?"*

"Like what?"

"Calm," she said. *"Certain."*

Ajah's expression shifted slightly, not losing steadiness but revealing something beneath it.

"No," he said. *"I just learned how to sit with things instead of trying to outrun them."*

Kia studied him, not as something separate, but as something possible, and for the first time that didn't make her feel behind—it made her feel open.

The sun lowered gradually, no urgency, just movement. Kia stood, not reluctant, not rushing.

"I'll see you again?" The question came before she shaped it.

Ajah looked at her, steady. *"You already know where to find me."*

She nodded, because she did.

As she walked away, her steps felt different—not lighter, not transformed, but aligned, and somewhere between the language she was learning and the quiet she was allowing, Kia realized something she had never permitted herself to believe: she was not just surviving her past.

She was beginning to understand herself beyond it, and in that understanding, something new was forming—not fast, not overwhelming, but steady.

The kind of connection that doesn't rush to define itself—but makes itself known anyway.

ChapterThirteen: The Sound of What He Survived

By the time Kia returned to Central Park that week, she no longer questioned why her body led her there.

She accepted it.

There were places in her life that required effort—rooms where she had to measure her tone, adjust her posture, anticipate the emotional temperature before stepping fully inside, spaces where she still entered with part of herself held back, waiting to see what version of the atmosphere would greet her—but the park had never asked that of her. It did not demand explanation or punish stillness, did not require performance.

It simply existed, wide, open, steady in the way certain truths are steady—without announcement, without insistence, without asking anyone to name them before they can be felt—and lately that had begun to feel like grace.

The air carried a deeper chill that afternoon, the kind that settled into the skin without biting, resting there long enough to be noticed, reminding her that the season was turning whether anyone acknowledged it or not.

Leaves brushed against the ground in soft, uneven rhythms, collecting in edges of paths and around the bases of benches as if the wind had arranged them there and then moved on.

The city hummed just beyond the trees, but from here it felt further away than usual, less like pressure and more like memory.

She heard the music before she saw him, but this time it was different.

It wasn't the piano, not first. It was the guitar—low, soulful, worn in a way that felt like history rather than age.

Each note carried weight, not heavy, not burdened, but lived through, shaped by something that had not always been gentle.

The sound didn't spread the way piano did; it gathered, stayed closer to the body, moved like something spoken in confidence rather than offered to a room.

Kia slowed, not out of hesitation, but out of recognition.

Ajah sat angled slightly away from the main path, the guitar resting against his body like something familiar, something trusted enough not to be performed with.

His fingers moved with the same ease she had seen at the piano, but the sound—this sound—held something deeper, more private, more exposed, less composed in the ways composition usually meant control.

The bench beside him held a light dusting of leaves.

Sunlight, thinner now than it had been a few weeks ago, filtered through the trees and landed across one side of his shoulder, across the neck of the guitar, across the ground between them in broken patterns that shifted every time the branches moved.

She didn't sit right away.

She stood there first, allowing the music to reach her fully, to move through her without interruption.

It settled low in her chest, pulling something loose that didn't hurt, but didn't feel light either. It felt true.

When she finally sat down, he didn't stop playing. He didn't look up, but the music shifted, not dramatically, just enough, as if her presence had entered it and been accounted for.

She listened longer this time, not watching his hands, not studying posture, not trying to decode the shape of him through observation, just listening, letting the sound do what it needed to do without asking it to become anything else.

The guitar moved differently than the piano had ever moved.

The notes bent at the edges.

They carried the faint scrape of finger against string, the soft friction of callus and wood and metal, the closeness of something made by touch rather than distance.

It was less architectural, more intimate.

When he finished, the silence that followed felt different than it had before—not complete, not resolved, open.

Kia sat inside it for a moment, then spoke. *"You don't play that the same way you play the piano."*

Ajah rested his hand lightly against the strings, stilling them completely before he answered.

"No," he said. *"I don't."*

Kia leaned forward slightly, her curiosity not pressing, but present. *"Why?"*

He didn't answer right away, not because he didn't have one, but because he chose when to give it.

He shifted slightly, setting the guitar aside with care before resting his forearms on his knees, his hands loosely clasped.

His gaze lowered just enough to suggest he was not avoiding her—he was going inward.

"Piano is structure," he said. *"It holds things in place."*

Kia nodded slowly. That made sense immediately.

The piano had always felt like that with him—measured, architectural, ordered without being cold, something built to carry weight without showing strain.

"And the guitar?"

Ajah exhaled softly. *"The guitar don't hold nothing,"* he said. *"It lets it out."*

The words settled into her, not as explanation, but as experience.

Kia studied him for another beat, something in her chest tightening, not from discomfort, but from recognition.

She knew the difference he meant before she fully understood why she knew it.

There were parts of her life that had been about holding, and parts that had only ever wanted a way out.

"That piece..." she began, then paused. *"It felt like something happened inside it."*

Ajah let out a quiet breath, something almost like a laugh, but not quite. *"It did."*

The air shifted then, not in the weather, but between them.

Kia didn't push, didn't lean in, didn't rescue the moment by filling it. She waited.

Ajah glanced up at her then, his gaze steady but different than before—not just present, but choosing.

"You ever hear something before you understand it?" he asked.

Kia nodded. *"All the time."*

He tilted his head slightly, considering her answer as if he knew exactly what it meant to someone like her.

"That's how I learned music," he said. *"Not reading it. Not studying it first. Hearing it."*

He leaned back slightly, posture still relaxed, but his voice carrying something deeper now, less surface, more memory.

"My grandmother used to play," he continued. *"Church piano. Nothing fancy. Just... steady."*

Kia listened closely, body still, attention fully anchored to him.

"She didn't teach me the way people think of teaching," he said. *"She just let me sit there. Let me hear it. Let me feel it."*

His gaze drifted slightly past Kia, not losing her, but touching something behind her, some earlier room, some earlier version of himself that still lived close enough to be reached.

"Said if I could feel where the sound was going, my hands would figure out how to follow it."

Kia felt that settle into her chest, because it sounded like something bigger than music—like trust, like instinct, like surviving the absence of language by learning how to hear what moved underneath it.

"Did they?" she asked softly.

Ajah smiled faintly. *"Eventually."*

The quiet stretched between them again, but this time it carried something fuller, warmer.

The park moved around them without intrusion—a jogger passed in the distance, a dog barked once and then lost interest, leaves slid across the path in a soft scrape that sounded almost like paper shifting on a desk—and none of it broke the moment, it only held its edges.

Kia hesitated before speaking again, her voice softer now, more careful.

"You said the guitar lets things out," she said. *"What was that?"*

Ajah's expression didn't close, but it shifted—not guarded, measured. He looked down at his hands for a moment, then back at her.

"Loss," he said simply.

The word landed clean, unadorned, heavy in its simplicity.

Kia didn't move, didn't react outwardly, but something inside her recognized it immediately.

"Who?" she asked, not intrusive, not demanding, present.

Ajah inhaled slowly, breath steady but deliberate. *"My mother."*

The park didn't change, but the space between them did.

The answer settled into the air with a weight that didn't need dramatic framing to matter.

Kia felt it low in her body first, the way certain truths arrived—not in thought, but in pressure.

"I was young," he continued. *"Old enough to remember. Too young to understand what I was losing."*

Kia's chest tightened slightly, her body leaning toward the story without meaning to.

"She used to sing," he said. *"Not like performance. Just... in the house. In the kitchen. While she moved through things."*

His voice softened, not out of sentimentality, but because memory sometimes required a different surface to stand on.

"That kind of singing stays with you different."

Kia swallowed, because she understood that—not exactly, not in the shape of his life, but in the way domestic sound could mark a person permanently, in the way a voice in a room could become part of the room long after it stopped.

"When she got sick," he continued, *"the house got quiet."*

He paused, his jaw tightening just slightly before releasing. *"Not peaceful quiet,"* he added. *"Empty quiet."*

Kia felt that distinction deeply, because she had known both—quiet that waited, quiet that threatened, quiet that held, quiet that hollowed.

"That's when I started playing more," he said. *"Trying to fill something that wasn't coming back."*

The truth of that didn't need explanation, didn't need decoration; it already held everything it needed.

Kia exhaled slowly, her voice quieter now, more vulnerable than she had intended. *"Did it help?"*

Ajah nodded once.

"Not the way I thought it would," he said. *"But enough."*

They sat there for a moment, the weight of what had been shared settling into something that didn't feel heavy. It felt honest.

Kia looked down at her hands, her fingers tracing the edge of her sleeve the way they did when she was thinking, when she was feeling something she hadn't fully named yet.

"I think I've been doing that too."

Ajah glanced at her. *"Doing what?"*

She hesitated, not because she didn't want to say it, but because saying it would make it real.

"Filling things," she said. *"With acting. With noise. With... anything that keeps me from sitting in it too long."*

Ajah nodded slowly, not in agreement, but in understanding. *"That's human."*

Kia looked up at him, something in her expression searching. *"Is it healthy?"*

He considered that for a moment, then shook his head slightly.

"Depends on whether you ever come back."

The words landed deeper than she expected, because they connected directly to something she had already begun to fear—not just the stage, not just the roles, but the thin place between expression and disappearance.

"I didn't come back the other night," she admitted, her voice soft, but steady.

Ajah didn't ask for clarification. He already understood.

"You did," he said. *"You just needed help finding your way."*

Kia felt something shift in her chest then, not dramatic, not overwhelming, but real, because no one had ever framed it that way before—not as failure, not as loss of control, but as something that could be navigated.

The sun dipped lower, the light softening around them, the air cooling just enough to make the moment feel held in time without freezing it.

The trees darkened by degrees, the city beyond the park growing more golden at the edges.

Kia stood slowly, her body grounded in a way that felt unfamiliar but welcome.

"Thank you."

Ajah looked at her, expression unchanged, gaze steady. *"For what?"*

She paused, searching for the right words, then let the search go.

"For not trying to fix it."

He nodded once. *"It don't need fixing,"* he said. *"It needs understanding."*

Kia let that sit, because it felt true in a way she hadn't allowed herself to believe before.

As she walked away, the sound of the guitar returned behind her, soft, steady, grounded in something deeper than performance, and for the first time she didn't feel like she had to outrun anything.

She felt like she could turn back if she needed to, and someone would still be there.

Chapter Fourteen: The Shape of What She Carried

She carried his words with her longer than she expected.

They did not settle immediately, did not resolve themselves into something she could organize or name.

They stayed—low, steady, present in the way certain truths remain after they've been spoken, shaping the silence that follows them.

His voice, the way he had said it, the simplicity of it, the weight beneath it—it did not leave her untouched.

By the time she returned to the park, she was not arriving empty.

The air had shifted again by the time Kia returned to the park, not just in temperature, but in weight.

There are days when the body arrives before the mind has agreed to follow, days when something inside begins to surface long before it has language, when the chest carries a pressure that isn't exactly pain but isn't light either, and all you can do is move toward the one place that has proven it can hold you without asking you to explain yourself first.

That was how she walked into Central Park that afternoon—not searching, not avoiding, not trying to outrun anything, but carrying something that had grown too large to remain unnamed.

The trees stood darker now, the green thinning into deeper shades as the season turned in quiet increments.

The path held the soft scrape of dry leaves shifting against concrete. Somewhere in the distance, a dog barked once and then lost interest.

The city was still there, still humming beyond the park's edges, but from where she entered it sounded dulled, like pressure wrapped in cloth.

Ajah was already there—not at the piano, not with the guitar in his hands.

He sat quietly on the bench, elbows resting loosely on his knees, his gaze fixed somewhere ahead, not distant, not withdrawn, not lost, just still, waiting without making it look like waiting.

Kia slowed when she saw him, not because she was unsure, but because she felt seen before she had said anything.

That happened with him more often now—not because he searched her out or studied her too hard or tried to anticipate what she hadn't offered, but because he simply noticed what she did not yet know how to conceal, and he noticed it without using it against her.

"You didn't bring the music today," she said, her voice softer than usual.

Ajah turned his head slightly, his eyes settling on her with the same calm they always carried, not questioning her tone, not reaching to fill it. *"Didn't feel like I needed it."*

Kia nodded slowly. That made sense—more than she wanted it to.

She sat beside him, closer than before, not touching, but near enough that the quiet between them felt shared rather than separate.

For a while, neither of them spoke, and for once the silence didn't ask her to perform inside it.

It didn't ask her to become articulate or brave or clear before she was ready.

It did not demand entry.

It simply waited.

Kia rested her hands in her lap, fingers loosely intertwined, her thumb moving absently against her skin the way it did when she was holding something she had not fully decided to release yet.

Her breathing wasn't uneven, but it wasn't easy either.

Each inhale brushed up against whatever sat beneath her ribs, whatever had followed her into the park and refused to stay nameless.

She inhaled slowly, then again, trying to find the place where words could form without tearing through her too quickly.

"My mother..."

The words came out before she could soften them, and she stopped, not because she didn't want to continue, but because saying them at all had already changed something.

The moment her mother entered the space between them, the air altered—not sharply, but enough.

The shape of the afternoon shifted around the truth that had finally been invited in.

Ajah didn't turn right away, didn't interrupt, but his presence adjusted subtly, intentionally.

His body angled just enough more toward her to let her know he was fully there without crowding what she was trying to say.

Kia swallowed, her throat tightening in a way that felt familiar but no longer overwhelming. *"She wasn't always…"*

She paused again, searching, not for a gentle version, but for an honest one. *"She wasn't always one person."*

That sentence landed differently than anything else she had said, because it did not explain, did not cushion, did not translate her experience into something easier to receive.

It told the truth.

Ajah's brow shifted slightly, not in confusion, but in recognition of the weight of what she had just named.

He didn't rush to define it, didn't reach for labels to organize what had been lived before it was ever studied. He let her continue.

Kia exhaled slowly, her shoulders dropping just enough for the next part to come through.

"There were days she was soft," she said. *"Quiet. Focused. She would cook, clean, move through the house like everything was in order."*

Her voice changed as she spoke, softening not out of performance but because memory had moved somewhere gentler.

"She would braid my hair sometimes," she added. *"Not talking much. Just... there."*

The memory didn't hurt—not at first. That was part of what made it difficult.

The tenderness had been real too, the softness, the days where the house held itself together, the moments where her mother's hands moved through her hair with patience and care, dividing, smoothing, braiding as if the world outside them could be kept out for a while.

"And then there were days..."

Her breath caught slightly, not sharply, but enough. She pressed her fingers together in her lap, grounding herself in the present before going on.

"It was like something changed inside her," she said. *"Fast. Without warning. Her voice would get louder. Faster. Her thoughts didn't... line up."*

he frowned, frustration flickering across her face, not at her mother, but at the impossibility of explaining something that had never made sense while it was happening.

"She would accuse my father of things that weren't real," she continued. *"Say people were watching her. Listening. That something was happening that we couldn't see."*

Ajah remained still, but his presence deepened, not heavy, not intrusive, grounded.

"And then it would escalate," Kia said, her voice lower now.

"The yelling. The pacing. The way she would move through the house like she was trying to outrun something inside her own head."

Her eyes dropped to her hands again. *"And we would have to adjust. Me and my father."*

That settled hard, because it wasn't only what happened—it was what they had to become because of it.

The daily recalibration.

The way she learned to read the room before entering it.

The way he learned to anchor what he could while she learned how not to disturb what might already be on the edge of breaking.

"He never left," she added quietly.

Ajah's gaze shifted.

That mattered.

Kia nodded faintly, her expression tightening, not with sadness alone, but with something more layered—love, confusion, reverence, unfinished questioning.

"He stayed through all of it," she said. *"Through the good days. Through the bad days.*

Through the days when she didn't even recognize what she was doing."

Her voice softened further.

"He would explain things to me," she continued. *"Not in big words. Not in ways that made it... heavy. Just enough so I wouldn't think it was my fault."*

Ajah let out a quiet breath, not interrupting, but acknowledging.

Kia looked up then, meeting his eyes for the first time since she began.

"But I still felt it."

There it was—the part explanation never fully touched, the part that remained in the body after language had done what it could.

"I still felt like I had to be careful," she said. *"Like I had to read the room before I spoke. Like I had to keep things calm so nothing would... shift."*

Her voice tightened slightly.

"Like if I moved wrong, said the wrong thing, felt too much—something would break."

Ajah's gaze didn't leave hers, and in that, something inside her steadied.

He was not looking at her like she was fragile, not looking like he needed to solve anything before she could continue.

He was simply staying where she had finally chosen to stand.

"That's where the acting came from," she said.

The realization did not feel new, but saying it aloud made it real in a different way.

"It wasn't just something I liked," she continued.

"It was something I needed."

Her breath deepened slightly, her body releasing tension she hadn't realized was still coiled in her shoulders.

"Because onstage, I could feel everything, and nothing would fall apart because of it."

The truth of that settled between them, unchallenged, uncorrected.

Ajah nodded slowly. *"That makes sense."*

Kia blinked, not because she expected disagreement, but because she had braced for it anyway.

"You don't think that's... unhealthy?"

The question came out smaller than she intended, more exposed.

Ajah leaned back slightly, posture still relaxed, his voice carrying a steadiness that did not try to soften the truth. *"It kept you safe,"* he said.

"That's not unhealthy."

He paused, then added, *"But you not there no more."*

The words didn't push her.

They didn't accuse her of being late to her own healing.

They invited consideration, space, a possibility she hadn't fully allowed herself to stand inside.

Kia inhaled slowly, her chest rising deeper now. *"I don't know how to turn it off,"* she admitted.

Ajah shook his head slightly. *"You don't turn it off."*

She frowned. *"Then what do I do?"*

He looked at her, not just seeing her, but holding her in a way that did not require her to shift or adjust or become easier to understand. *"You learn when to step out."*

The distinction landed—clear, not easy, but clear.

Kia exhaled softly, her shoulders lowering just enough for her body to register the difference between resolution and direction.

This was not resolution, but it was direction.

The quiet returned, but it wasn't empty—it was full.

After a while, Kia spoke again, more softly now, more honestly. *"I used to think love meant staying no matter what."*

Ajah didn't interrupt.

"Watching my father," she continued, *"the way he stayed, the way he held everything together, I thought that was what it was supposed to look like."*

Her voice shifted, not rejecting what she'd seen, but questioning its completeness.

"But I don't know if I understand it completely."

Ajah nodded once. *"You understand what you saw."*

Kia looked at him, waiting.

"You still learning what it feel like," he added.

The words didn't rush her.

They gave her room—room to let love be more than endurance, more than containment, more than staying because leaving would break something, room to imagine it as presence that did not erase the weight, but did not require her to carry it alone either.

Kia sat there, body grounded, breath steadier than when she arrived, mind quieter—not empty, but clear—and for the first time she didn't feel like what she had lived through needed to be repaired before it could be understood.

It could simply be held, and in that holding something shifted, not dramatically, not all at once, but enough—enough for her to recognize something she had never fully allowed herself to believe.

She was not alone inside what she carried.

And the man sitting beside her was not trying to change it.

He was choosing to understand it with her.

Chapter Fifteen: The Space Between Staying and Wanting More

What she shared with him did not leave her where she had been.

It stayed with her—not heavy, not overwhelming, but present in a way that reshaped how she moved through the quiet that followed.

Saying it out loud had not emptied it. If anything, it had given it form, something she could feel without needing to hold it all inside her body at once.

The way he had listened, the way he had not interrupted or softened or tried to redirect what she had lived through—it did not disappear when she left him.

It stayed, steady, working its way through her in ways she was only beginning to understand.

By the time she returned to the park again, she was not carrying the same weight.

It had shifted—not gone, not resolved, but different in how it sat inside her.

It did not happen all at once.

That would have been easier—easier to name, easier to manage, easier to resist.

What grew between Kia and Ajah did not arrive like a moment.

It did not announce itself with revelation or force itself into language before either of them was ready to carry it.

It unfolded the way certain truths unfolded—quietly, steadily, as something that had been forming long before anyone chose to look directly at it.

By then, the park had become its own kind of rhythm—not routine, not obligation, not habit in the dull sense of the word, but something softer, something chosen.

Kia no longer wondered whether he would be there, and he no longer looked surprised when she was.

They met inside that space the way two people meet inside a language that does not need translation—pauses understood, silences shared, presence offered without negotiation or explanation.

Nothing between them had been declared, and yet nothing felt uncertain in the ways uncertainty usually did. It was not confusion. It was unfolding.

But something had changed—not in the way they spoke, but in the way they felt what was not being said.

That afternoon the air carried warmth again, the kind that lingered just long enough to remind the body that seasons could soften after holding cold for too long.

Light moved differently through the trees, less brittle now, more fluid, laying itself across the path in shifting pieces as the branches stirred overhead.

The grass held a deeper green after the last stretch of gray, and the city beyond the park felt distant enough to blur into sound rather than pressure.

Kia walked slower than usual, not because she was tired, but because she was aware—of her breath, of her steps, of the quiet anticipation settling beneath her skin in a way that made her conscious of herself from the inside out.

The way her stomach tightened slightly when she crossed the familiar path.

The way her chest seemed to know she was nearing him before her eyes confirmed it.

The way expectation, when it was not fear, could still feel like trembling.

She saw him before she heard the music.

Ajah stood beside the piano, adjusting something near its base, his movements deliberate, unhurried, practiced in a way that had long since stopped feeling impressive and had begun to feel intimate instead.

There was something grounding in watching someone handle an object they knew thoroughly, something almost private about competence when it wasn't being displayed for approval.

Kia paused for a moment before approaching—not out of hesitation, but out of recognition.

She was no longer just coming to listen. She was coming for him.

That truth did not arrive in language first.

It arrived in the body—in the small pause she gave herself before stepping forward, in the way her breathing changed, in the way seeing him standing there seemed to settle something and stir something else at the same time.

"You're early," he said without turning.

Kia smiled despite herself. *"You always know that."*

He glanced back at her then, the corner of his mouth lifting just enough to acknowledge the pattern between them.

"You don't walk the same when you're not thinking."

She raised an eyebrow. *"That sounds like observation."*

He nodded. *"It is."*

There was ease in the exchange, but not casualness. Ease was what happened when two people had already spent enough time in each other's presence to stop performing familiarity and begin living inside it.

She stepped closer, her presence settling beside him more naturally now, her body no longer measuring distance the way it once had.

She could feel the quiet heat rising from the piano's dark surface where the sun had touched it, could hear the faint clink of whatever he was tightening near the base, could smell the mix of metal, wood, air, and the clean trace of his cologne when the wind shifted just enough to carry it toward her.

"So what does it say?" she asked.

Ajah rested one hand lightly against the piano, considering her question with the same care he gave most things.

"That you're not here for the music today."

The words landed softly, but directly.

Kia held his gaze for a moment longer than she normally would have—not challenging, not deflecting, just there.

"Maybe I'm not."

The air between them shifted, not dramatically, but enough.

Ajah didn't move, didn't step closer, didn't step back, but something in his stillness changed—less neutral now, more aware of what stood between them and what did not.

"Then what are you here for?"

The question was not heavy, but it carried weight, because it asked her to name something she had only just begun to feel clearly enough to admit to herself.

Kia exhaled slowly, her chest rising, her breath steady but intentional.

She could have turned it into a joke, could have made it lighter than it felt, could have protected herself with vagueness and called that caution.

But she didn't.

"I think I'm trying to figure that out."

Ajah nodded once, not pressing, but not releasing the moment either.

"That's honest."

She laughed softly, and this time the nervousness did not hide inside it; it moved with it.

"It's also inconvenient."

A small smile touched his face.

"Most real things are."

The quiet that followed did not stretch uncomfortably. It deepened.

Kia moved to sit on the bench, her body settling into a space that no longer felt borrowed, her hands resting loosely in her lap, her attention no longer split between past and present but fully anchored in the moment in front of her.

Ajah joined her after a moment, sitting close enough that the space between them felt chosen—not accidental, not careless, but intentional in its restraint.

The bench was warm where sunlight had rested on it. A breeze moved through the leaves overhead, scattering light across the ground in slow, restless patterns.

Somewhere off to the left, a child laughed and then ran out of sight. The city hummed at the edges without pressing inward.

"Do you ever think about what this is?" Kia asked.

The question came out softer than she expected, more vulnerable.

Ajah leaned forward slightly, forearms resting on his knees, his gaze directed ahead but aware of her beside him.

"Sometimes."

Kia turned her head, studying his profile—the line of his jaw, the quiet in his posture, the way he seemed to inhabit himself fully without tightening around it. *"And?"*

He exhaled slowly. His answer did not rush toward her.

It arrived when it was ready.

"I think it's something that don't need to be rushed into a name."

She nodded, because part of her agreed, but another part wanted shape, wanted certainty, wanted the relief of definition.

"That sounds safe."

Ajah turned toward her then, meeting her eyes fully.

"It is." Then, after a beat, *"And it's also honest."*

Kia felt both parts of that—the safety, the honesty, the relief of not being pulled, and the ache of not yet knowing exactly where something real was headed.

"I don't know if I've ever had something that just... existed without pressure," she admitted.

Ajah's expression softened slightly, not out of pity, but out of recognition.

"That don't mean you don't deserve it."

The words settled into her, not dramatically, but deeply, like water reaching something in the soil that had been dry too long to know how to ask.

Kia looked down at her hands again, her fingers tracing slow patterns against her skin, the same unconscious movement she made whenever she was standing near a truth she hadn't fully opened yet.

"I think I'm starting to rely on this."

Ajah didn't react immediately, but his posture shifted—more attentive now.

"On what?"

She hesitated, not because she didn't know, but because saying it aloud would give it form.

"This space," she said. *"These conversations. You."*

The honesty in it did not come with apology, but it carried awareness.

She knew what she was saying, knew what she was risking by letting it enter the air between them without disguise, knew that dependence, when it had been shaped by survival, could borrow the language of closeness too easily.

Ajah sat with it, his gaze steady, his breathing even. When he spoke, his voice remained calm, but something in it carried more firmness now.

"That's where you gotta be careful."

Kia's head lifted slightly, not defensive, but alert. *"Why?"*

He turned more fully toward her, voice grounded in a truth he was not interested in softening into comfort.

"Because healing and attachment can start to feel the same."

The words landed clean, clear. Kia felt her chest tighten slightly, not with resistance, but with recognition. *"And they're not?"*

Ajah shook his head gently. *"They can overlap, but they not the same thing."*

That distinction settled into the space between them like something precise enough to cut and careful enough not to wound if held correctly.

Kia looked at him, the question still present in her. *"So what is this?"*

This time, the question held more than curiosity. It held feeling.

Ajah studied her for a moment, his gaze steady, his presence unchanged—but something beneath it revealing itself just enough to be felt.

"It's something real."

Kia swallowed, because that was enough—and also not enough. There are truths that satisfy the heart before they satisfy the mind. This was one of them.

"And real can grow into something more," he added quietly.

The air shifted again, softer now, but heavier.

Kia felt it in her breath, in her chest, in the almost-imperceptible way her body leaned toward him without fully closing the space between them.

"Does that scare you?" she asked.

Ajah didn't hesitate. *"No."* Then, after a pause, *"But it makes me pay attention."*

Kia let out a slow breath, her shoulders lowering slightly, her body easing into something she had not allowed herself to feel fully before, because this was different—not chaotic, not unpredictable, not something she had to manage before it shifted, but also not something she could control. That realization didn't push her away.

It drew her closer, not physically yet, but inwardly.

She leaned back slightly, her gaze lifting toward the trees, the light filtering through them in patterns that felt almost deliberate, as if the day itself had slowed down enough to witness what was happening between them without interrupting it.

"I don't want to lose this."

Ajah's voice came steady, grounded.

"Then don't rush it into something it's not ready to be."

Kia nodded slowly, because that felt right, even if it was not easy, even if wanting more had already begun to move inside her in ways she could no longer pretend not to feel.

The space between them remained, but it no longer felt like distance.

It felt like possibility.

And for the first time in her life, Kia understood something that did not come from survival, adaptation, or performance, but from presence.

Love did not have to arrive loudly to be real.

Sometimes it arrived quietly and asked you to stay long enough to recognize it.

Chapter Sixteen: When Silence Meant Something Different

What he said did not leave her the way the others had.

It stayed—clear, precise, not loud, not forceful, but settled into her in a way that did not allow her to dismiss it or reshape it into something easier to carry.

She had wanted honesty. She had asked for it without saying the words directly.

And when it came, it did not arrive in comfort. It arrived in clarity.

That difference followed her long after she left the park, long after the sound of the piano had faded into distance, long after the evening had settled into the quiet of her room.

By the time she returned again, nothing had been resolved.

Not inside her. Not between them.

And maybe that was the point.

It didn't begin with a fight. That would have been easier—easier to recognize, easier to respond to, easier to fix.

What shifted between Kia and Ajah began quietly, so quietly it almost went unnoticed until it had already changed the way they stood near each other, the way her body registered him before he spoke, the way the park itself seemed to hold its breath around them.

The day looked like any other on its surface. The park was the same—the light, the air, the rhythm of people moving through their own lives without interruption.

Joggers passed in practiced silence, headphones on, bodies committed to movement.

A dog barked once near the path, then settled. Leaves moved in small, dry scrapes across the pavement when the wind found them.

The city remained where it always was—just beyond the trees, humming, layered, unbothered.

But Kia felt it the moment she stepped into the space.

Something was off. Not loud. Not visible. Not anything she could have pointed to if someone had asked. But her body knew before her thoughts did.

That old internal tightening returned—not fully, not with the violence of childhood, but enough to register.

Her shoulders drew in just slightly. Her breath shortened and then corrected itself. Her pace slowed, not because she chose to slow it, but because some part of her had already begun listening more closely than usual.

Ajah was at the piano. His hands moved across the keys with the same precision, the same patience, the same control she had come to know as part of him, but the music didn't reach. It stayed near him, contained, structured, closed in a way she had never heard from him before.

Usually, his music made room. It opened. It met her before she sat down. It adjusted without announcing that it had felt her arrive.

This didn't. This remained with itself.

Kia stood there longer than usual, waiting for the familiar shift—for the slight softening in phrasing, the subtle acknowledgment that he knew she was there. It didn't come.

A breeze moved through the trees, carrying the cooler edge of late afternoon across her face.

The bench nearest him caught the light in narrow slants through the branches overhead.

Somewhere behind her, two students laughed at something she couldn't hear clearly.

The normalcy of everything around her made the change feel sharper. She walked closer, measured, composed, her body already adjusting to something she couldn't yet name.

He didn't stop playing, didn't look up, didn't shift. The distance between them remained, and for the first time, it felt like distance.

Kia sat down slowly, her hands resting in her lap, her posture composed, her expression neutral in a way that took effort she had not needed before.

She listened, not because she wanted to, but because she was trying to understand what had changed. The piece ended.

Ajah's hands lifted from the keys. The silence that followed did not hold the same warmth it once had.

It didn't open. It didn't welcome. It simply sat there—finished, contained, self-sufficient.

"You're early."

The same words. Different tone.

Kia nodded once. *"I had time."*

He adjusted something along the side of the piano, fingers precise, movements deliberate but detached. *"That's good."*

The conversation didn't move forward. It stopped there. And in that stillness, Kia felt it clearly—not imagined, not projected. Something had pulled back.

She studied him for a moment, her gaze steady, her thoughts already moving through possibilities too quickly—something she'd said, something she'd missed, something she'd done without realizing it.

That old instinct returned with unnerving speed. *Find it. Fix it. Don't let it shift too far.*

"Did I do something?"

Ajah paused. Not long, but long enough. He turned slightly toward her, expression held in place—not closed, not open, just measured. *"No."*

Kia felt the answer, not just the word, but the space behind it. *"That didn't sound like no."*

Ajah exhaled slowly, his shoulders shifting just slightly, his gaze lowering for a moment before returning to hers. *"It's not about something you did."*

Her chest tightened, because that wasn't clarity. That was distance in another form. *"Then what is it about?"*

He didn't answer immediately, not because he didn't know, but because he was choosing how to say something he did not want to weaponize.

The wind moved again, lifting a few leaves from the ground and sending them across the path in a soft, scraping line.

A child called out in the distance. The world continued around them, but the bench had become its own contained weather.

"You said something the other day," he said finally.

Kia frowned slightly. *"I say a lot of things."*

He nodded once. *"You said you were starting to rely on this... on me."*

The memory landed immediately—clear, undeniable. Kia sat up slightly, her body reacting before her words did. *"I was being honest."*

Ajah nodded again. *"I know."*

The calm in his voice did not soothe her. It unsettled her more, because it sounded like he had already thought this through, already stood somewhere she had not yet reached, already drawn a boundary she had not known was forming.

"Then why does that feel like a problem?"

He turned fully toward her now, posture still grounded, presence more direct.

"Because I don't want to become something you need to feel stable."

The words landed harder than she expected, not because they were cruel, but because they were careful. And careful truths were sometimes harder to argue with than careless ones.

Kia felt something move inside her—not anger at first, something closer to rejection, to exposure, to the sudden humiliation of having offered something honest and hearing caution in return.

"That's not what I said," she replied, her voice tightening just slightly.

Ajah held her gaze. *"That's what it can turn into."*

Kia looked away, her eyes dropping to her hands, fingers pressing together more firmly now, breath shortening despite her effort to keep it even.

The bench beneath her felt harder suddenly, the air cooler, the whole park seeming to have taken one step back from her without moving.

"So what—you want me to just not feel anything?"

He shook his head. *"That's not what I'm saying."*

"Then what are you saying?"

The question came sharper this time, less managed.

The old edge of performance entered her voice, not because she was acting, but because she was hurt enough that precision returned in place of softness.

Ajah's expression shifted slightly, not defensive, firmer.

"I'm saying we need to keep this grounded," he said. *"Not let it become something that replaces the work you're doing."*

Kia let out a short breath, something between a laugh and the first release of frustration. *"You think I'm using you?"*

Ajah didn't answer right away, and that was the answer.

Kia stood, not abruptly, but decisively. Her chest was tight now, her thoughts moving faster, emotion rising with the familiar sensation of something important shifting before she had control over it.

"That's not fair."

Ajah remained seated, posture steady, voice calm. *"I didn't say you were doing it on purpose."*

Kia shook her head, her hands moving slightly as if they needed to release something her mouth could not hold. *"That doesn't make it better."*

The space between them changed again.

This time it widened, not because either of them moved far, but because meaning had entered it.

Ajah watched her. His face did not close, did not retreat, but neither did it reach.

"I'm trying to be honest with you."

Kia nodded once, too quickly. *"So am I."*

The words sat there, unresolved. For the first time since she had met him, Kia did not feel anchored in his presence.

She felt unsteady—not because he had changed into someone unsafe, but because something in her had been touched, and it hurt.

The pain was not dramatic. It did not come as tears or anger alone. It came as recognition, as the sudden return of a body-memory she had been working so hard to loosen from.

That old internal scramble—the need to understand immediately, to repair quickly, to locate what had shifted and stop it from becoming loss.

"I think I need some space," she said finally.

Ajah nodded, not arguing, not stopping her. *"That might be a good idea."*

The agreement did not comfort her.

It confirmed what her body had already feared—that even steadiness could alter, that even something gentle could set a boundary she had not prepared for.

Kia turned. Her steps stayed controlled, but her chest remained tight, breath uneven now in a way she had not felt in weeks.

The path ahead of her looked the same. The trees had not changed. The light was still breaking through leaves in the same places.

But the park no longer felt the way it had when she arrived—not unsafe, but not the same.

As she walked away, the piano began again behind her—structured, contained, distant—and for the first time, it didn't reach her.

That night, standing in front of her mirror, Kia stared at her reflection longer than usual.

The room around her held its familiar quiet—the muted hum of distant traffic outside, the soft mechanical rattle of heat moving through old pipes, the slight creak of the floor when she shifted her weight.

None of it settled her.

Her face.

Her eyes.

Her posture.

She searched herself as if the answer might be visible somewhere she could point to.

She tried to locate the feeling, not the surface one, the deeper one.

It wasn't anger, not fully.

It was fear—not of him, but of what she had allowed herself to feel.

Because for the first time, something steady had entered her life... and it didn't belong to her.

She inhaled slowly, her breath catching before evening out.

"You're not a child," she said softly to her reflection.

But her voice didn’t fully believe it, because the part of her that had learned to read rooms, adjust quickly, protect stability before it broke had just been triggered, and now she didn’t know if she had stepped too far or finally stepped into something real.

Chapter Seventeen: The Distance That Taught Them What Stayed

The space she asked for did not disappear once she stepped into it.

It held.

Not sharply, not in a way that demanded attention every second, but in a quiet, steady way that followed her through the next morning, through the small movements of getting dressed, of gathering her things, of stepping into a day that did not feel broken but no longer felt the same either.

What had passed between them had not unraveled anything—it had revealed something, and now she had to sit with it without reaching for him to steady it.

The first day without him felt manageable.

Not easy, but contained. Kia moved through her routine with intention, her steps measured, her focus directed toward things that required her attention in ways that did not ask too much beyond presence.

Class. Notes. Hallways. Brief conversations that did not press inward. She answered when spoken to, listened when needed, responded when appropriate, and in between all of it, she avoided Central Park.

It wasn't a decision she announced to herself.

She never stood in front of a mirror and said she would stay away, never framed it as discipline or self-protection or principle.

It was something her body chose before her mind could argue with it, because the park no longer felt neutral.

It held something now, something unresolved. The path toward it existed in her the way certain habits lived in the body long before they were spoken aloud.

She would leave class and feel her steps wanting to tilt west without permission, her chest already anticipating the openness, the bench, the possibility of music, and then she would stop, turn elsewhere.

By the second day, the absence shifted, not dramatically, not in a way anyone else would have seen, but persistently.

She noticed it first in the smallest places—the way her eyes moved instinctively toward open stretches of city as if expecting to find him there without explanation, the way her ears caught distant notes—someone practicing piano in a residence hall, a guitarist on a corner, even a melody leaking from a passing car—and immediately sharpened, searching for the particular steadiness she had come to associate with him.

She never turned toward the sound. She kept walking.

Campus moved around her the way it always did—doors swinging open in uneven rhythms, students crossing paths with conversations half-finished, backpacks slung over shoulders like armor worn so casually no one called it that.

The afternoon light stretched longer now, catching on brick and glass and the metal handles of doors, making ordinary things look briefly more defined than they were, and still, something in her remained elsewhere.

In class, she found herself quieter than she had been in weeks, not withdrawn, not shut down, but internal.

The words that had once come with growing clarity now sat just beneath the surface, fully formed but reluctant to cross into speech.

She listened more, wrote more, let the discussion move around her while she stayed just outside its center.

Her professor noticed, not directly, not in a way that would embarrass or expose her, but in the slight extra second their gaze lingered on her when a question passed the room unanswered, in the way their voice softened just slightly when asking if anyone had more to add, in the subtle awareness of someone who knew a student had shifted but respected them enough not to force explanation.

That afternoon, she sat on the steps outside the building, her notebook open but untouched, her pen resting loosely between her fingers.

The stone beneath her still held a trace of warmth from the sun.

A group of students laughed too loudly half a landing below her. Someone walked past carrying coffee and the smell moved briefly through the air before disappearing.

She stared down at the sentence she had written days earlier.

It wasn't me.

The words looked different now, not wrong, incomplete.

Kia leaned back against the cool stone behind her, exhaling slowly as her shoulders lowered a fraction.

It wasn't me...

The thought lingered, then shifted.

But it is me now.

The realization did not hurt. It settled.

Because the part of her that had leaned into Ajah's presence, that had allowed herself to feel grounded in something outside of her own control—that part was not false.

It was not weakness.

It was not manipulation or confusion or some accidental slipping of boundaries she could dismiss once distance clarified things.

It was real, and losing access to it, even temporarily, revealed something she had not wanted to admit.

She missed him.

Not dramatically, not in a way that shattered her appetite or made her fail classes or stand crying under trees at dusk, but in a way that threaded quietly through the architecture of her day—in moments where she would have once turned toward the park without thinking, in the pause after hearing something insightful in class and knowing exactly where she would have carried it, in the strange lack of completion at the end of a thought that had grown used to another mind meeting it.

By the third day, she stopped avoiding the thought of the park, but she still didn't go.

Instead, she chose longer routes, paths that kept her moving without bringing her close enough to feel the pull of something she was not yet ready to face directly.

She walked streets she did not need to walk, circled blocks she could have cut through, let the city fill time for her without asking it to mean anything.

That night, standing in front of her mirror, she studied herself again, not searching for a role, not testing expressions, not checking whether she looked composed enough to pass as settled, just looking.

Her reflection didn't feel unfamiliar, but it didn't feel fully settled either.

The lamp beside her bed cast a soft amber light across one side of her face, leaving the other in gentler shadow.

Her room was quiet except for the distant hum of traffic and the occasional laughter that rose from somewhere down the hall and then faded.

"What are you actually afraid of?" she asked herself softly.

The question lingered, then slowly something surfaced.

"That he was right."

She didn't flinch from hearing it, because beneath the frustration, beneath the sting of feeling misunderstood, beneath the humiliation of hearing caution where she had offered honesty, there had been something else—recognition.

She had leaned into him, not strategically, not theatrically, not because she was trying to make him responsible for what she hadn't yet learned how to hold, but deeply, and that was new.

For the first time in her life, calm had not come only from what she built inside herself.

It had arrived through relation, through being met, through being mirrored in a space where she didn't have to do all the stabilizing alone, and when he pulled back, it exposed how much she had begun to depend on that.

Kia closed her eyes briefly, her breath steady but thoughtful.

"That doesn't mean it wasn't real."

Because it was. It still was, and that made the distance harder.

Across the city, Ajah sat alone in his apartment, the guitar resting against his leg, his fingers moving across the strings without urgency, without performance, without any intention beyond expression.

The room was quiet, not empty, but still. A lamp glowed low in the corner.

The window beside him reflected a softened version of the room back into itself while the city moved outside in fragments—headlights passing, windows lit and dimming, a siren far enough away to be atmosphere rather than intrusion.

He had not gone to the park that day, not because he didn't want to, but because he needed to sit with what had shifted.

The conversation replayed in his mind, not obsessively, not as self-punishment, not with the sharp repetition of regret, but with attention, the kind of attention he gave things he knew mattered enough to deserve being understood before they were acted on.

Her words. Her tone. The way her body had responded before she had spoken.

The way the space between them had changed the moment he named something she hadn't yet fully seen.

He let his fingers fall still against the strings.

The room deepened around the silence.

"You didn't handle that wrong," he said quietly to himself.

But the words did not settle as easily as he wanted them to, because being right didn't feel the same as being connected.

He leaned back slightly in his chair, his gaze drifting toward the window, the city stretching beyond it in a rhythm he had learned long ago how to move within without becoming lost inside.

He understood what he had said, believed it.

He knew too well what it meant for healing to disguise itself as attachment, for loneliness to attach meaning too quickly to whatever brought relief, for tenderness to become dependency if it was not held honestly, but he also understood something else.

She hadn't been wrong either.

What had grown between them had grown naturally, unforced, real.

There had been no manipulation in her honesty, no carelessness in her reaching, no attempt to use him, only feeling, and in trying to protect the foundation of what they had, he had created distance. Necessary, maybe, but still distance.

Ajah picked up the guitar again. His fingers moved more slowly this time, the sound softer, more reflective, each note landing closer to thought than melody.

He wasn't trying to fill anything. He was listening to what remained after the moment had passed, and what remained was not absence.

It was her, not physically, but undeniably—in the way the music shaped itself differently now, as if some part of him still played toward her even with no one there to hear it, in the way silence carried more weight than it had before, in the way his thoughts moved toward her without effort, not as fantasy, not as distraction, but as reality continuing in another place.

He paused, one hand resting lightly against the strings.

"You felt that."

Not a question. An acknowledgment, because he had felt it too, and that was the part he had not named out loud.

Back in her room, Kia sat on her bed with the notebook open again, pen finally moving after so many minutes of stillness.

She didn't write paragraphs, didn't try to structure herself into understanding, only one sentence.

I don't want to need him.

She stared at it, then added—*But I want him in my life.*

The distinction mattered more than she expected it to, because it separated hunger from choice, survival from desire, fear from truth.

It gave her something she had not always had—choice, not reaction, not adaptation, not the quick shaping of herself around whatever would keep the room from shifting.

Choice.

She closed the notebook slowly, breath steady, body settling into something that did not feel resolved, but clearer.

Across the city, Ajah stood and set the guitar aside, his movements deliberate, his mind quieter now than it had been when he first sat down.

He did not reach for his phone, did not move toward the door, did not try to erase distance before it had done what distance sometimes needed to do, because he understood something that had taken him years to learn.

Not all space meant separation.

Sometimes it meant allowing something real to find its shape without pressure.

And somewhere between them, without words, without presence, without certainty, something remained.

Not fragile.

Not broken.

Waiting.

Chapter Eighteen: The Way Back Was Chosen

What remained between them did not disappear in the space.

It clarified.

Not all at once, not in a way that demanded immediate return, but in the quiet unfolding of days where distance was allowed to do what it was meant to do—not sever, not erase, but reveal what could stand without constant contact.

What they had not named had not weakened. It had held. And somewhere inside that holding, something steadier than impulse began to take shape.

Kia didn't wake up missing him. She woke up knowing what she wanted to do. There was a difference.

Morning light stretched slowly across her room, soft and unintrusive, settling over her skin like something that did not require response.

It touched the edge of her notebook, the chair by the window, the floorboards near her bed—ordinary things made briefly gentle by the hour.

She lay there for a moment, eyes open, not chasing the thought, not testing it for weakness, not asking whether it would still feel true in five minutes.

She let it sit, and in sitting, it clarified. This was not impulse, not loneliness pretending to be certainty, not the ache of missing him dressed up as urgency.

It had weight. It had steadiness. And more than anything, it had choice.

She sat up slowly, her feet finding the floor with a steadiness she had not felt in days, her body no longer bracing against something unnamed.

The air felt different—not lighter, not easier, aligned. That was the word for it.

Not free of feeling, not absent tension, but aligned enough that her body and mind were no longer moving in separate directions.

She moved through her morning without distraction. Her actions were deliberate, unhurried, quiet in their own confidence.

Water running over her skin in the shower.

Steam rising and disappearing against the mirror. The sound of hangers shifting as she chose her clothes.

She pulled her hair back, studied herself for a moment, then let it fall again. She didn't need to prepare herself for him the way she might have once mistaken care for preparation.

This wasn't performance. This was presence.

By the time she stepped outside, the city had already found its rhythm. Cars moved in patient lines.

Sidewalks filled and emptied in patterns too old to need attention. A bus sighed at the corner.

Someone laughed too loudly across the street. Somewhere above it all, a window opened and music drifted down briefly before the block swallowed it.

Kia did not rush to match any of it. She moved within it—measured, grounded, aware. Each step toward Central Park felt intentional, not because she was rehearsing what to say, but because she wasn't.

She had spent enough of her life preparing for conversations that never went the way she planned, enough time trying to get ahead of tone, meaning, reaction, fracture, enough time shaping her words around possibility before they had even been spoken. This was not that.

When she reached the edge of the park, she paused, not out of hesitation, but out of acknowledgment.

The space in front of her held memory now, held tension, held the afterimage of distance and the ache of what had been left unsaid, but it held something else too—truth.

She stepped in.

Grass stretched wide and familiar, the open space carrying the kind of quiet she had come to understand not as emptiness, but as permission.

The trees moved lightly in the morning air, branches shifting just enough to make the light unstable in a beautiful way.

The path curved ahead in that same uninsistent way it always had, never asking where she was going, only receiving her when she came.

The piano was already there, positioned where it always was, grounded, waiting—not abandoned, not misplaced, exactly where it belonged, and so was he.

Ajah sat at the bench, his posture relaxed but attentive, his hands resting lightly near the keys, not playing yet. He looked up before she reached him, not surprised, not guarded, present.

Kia felt it immediately—the difference. The space between them was still there, but it no longer felt like distance.

She walked the rest of the way without slowing, her breath even, her shoulders relaxed, her gaze steady.

When she reached him, she didn't sit right away. She stood there for a moment, letting the reality of being in front of him again settle fully into her body.

No rush. No defense. No performance of ease. Just arrival.

"Hi."

Ajah's lips curved slightly, not a full smile, but something warmer than neutrality.

"Hi."

The simplicity of it grounded her more than anything else could have.

No dramatic opening. No emotional overcorrection. No need to pretend the distance had not happened or that it had meant less than it did.

She sat beside him then, her movements unhurried, her hands resting loosely in her lap, her body angled just slightly toward him, not leaning, not withdrawing, balanced.

For a moment, neither of them spoke, but this silence felt different.

It wasn't filled with tension. It held space.

Kia exhaled softly, her gaze dropping briefly to her hands before lifting again.

"I thought about what you said."

Ajah didn't interrupt, didn't shift. He listened.

"And I didn't like it," she added, her tone honest but not sharp.

He nodded once. *"I figured."*

A small breath escaped her, almost a laugh, but not quite. *"But I understood it,"* she continued.

That landed differently. Ajah's posture shifted just slightly, his attention sharpening—not defensive, not guarded, engaged.

Kia turned more fully toward him now, voice steady, words chosen but not rehearsed.

"I was leaning into this," she said. *"Into you. Not because I don't know how to stand on my own, but because for the first time... it felt safe not to have to do everything alone."*

The admission did not shake her voice. It strengthened it.

Ajah held her gaze, his expression open now in a way it had not been before.

"That's not something I want to take away from you," he said quietly.

Kia nodded.

"I know. But when you said it the way you did, it felt like you were stepping back from something we both felt."

The word *we* lingered between them, unavoidable, honest.

Ajah exhaled slowly, his gaze dropping for a moment before returning to hers.

"I was trying to protect the foundation, not pull away from the connection."

Kia studied him for a moment, letting the words land fully before she answered.

"Then say that," she said softly. *"Because what I heard... wasn't that."*

The honesty didn't create tension. It cleared it.

Ajah nodded, a small release moving through his shoulders, something loosening there.

"That's fair."

The acknowledgment settled between them like something real enough not to need decoration.

Kia felt it then—not the absence of tension, but the presence of understanding.

Not perfect resolution. Not easy repair. Understanding.

"I don't want to need you to feel okay," she said after a moment. *"But I do want you in my life. And I don't think those two things cancel each other out."*

Ajah's gaze softened, something deeper surfacing in his expression now, something less measured, more felt.

"They don't."

The words carried weight—agreement, recognition, relief, though neither of them named it.

For a while, they sat without speaking again, and this silence felt full.

Ajah turned slightly toward the piano, his fingers resting lightly against the keys, then pausing.

"Can I play something?"

Kia nodded, shoulders relaxing further.

"Please."

The first notes came softly, not familiar, not repeated, something new, something shaped by the distance they had crossed and the care with which they had chosen to return.

The melody moved with the same steadiness she had come to know in him, but this time there was something else inside it—openness without caution, tenderness without demand.

Kia closed her eyes, not to disappear into the music, but to feel it fully.

This time it didn't steady her because she needed it to. It met her where she already was.

Her breathing aligned with the rhythm, her body no longer bracing, her thoughts no longer pulling in different directions.

The bench beneath her stayed solid. The air touched her face lightly. Somewhere in the distance a child called out and then quieted.

Leaves moved overhead in a low, constant whisper. Nothing in her was trying to outrun anything.

She didn't lean into him. She didn't pull away. She stayed.

And when she opened her eyes, she didn't feel like she was returning to herself. She felt like she had never left.

Ajah finished the piece slowly, his hands lifting from the keys with intention, the final note lingering just long enough to make the silence afterward feel like continuation instead of end.

He turned back to her. For a moment, neither of them spoke, but something had shifted, not dramatically, not loudly, but undeniably.

Kia met his eyes, her expression softer now, her presence steady.

"That felt different."

Ajah nodded. *"It is."*

She tilted her head slightly, studying him.

"What changed?"

He held her gaze a moment longer before answering.

"We did."

The simplicity of it settled into her chest, not as something to analyze, not as a question she needed to solve, but as something true enough to accept before fully understanding its shape.

Kia smiled then, not wide, not performative, real.

And for the first time since the distance had opened between them, she didn't feel like she was trying to understand where she stood.

She knew.

Not everything. Not the future. Not the outcome.

But this—

This was real.

Grounded.

And growing.

Chapter Nineteen: The Space Between Them Changed First

What they chose the day before did not disappear once they left it.

It held.

Not loudly, not in a way that demanded constant attention, but in the quiet, steady presence of something that had been acknowledged without being forced into definition.

The return had not rushed them forward. It had settled them. And in that settling, something deeper than uncertainty had taken root—something that did not need to be questioned every moment to prove it was still there.

The shift didn't arrive as a confession. It didn't need to. Some things did not require language the moment they became true. Some things announced themselves first through the body—through ease, through awareness, through the sudden absence of effort where effort had once lived.

What had changed between Kia and Ajah had already moved past uncertainty.

It had not become named, not fully, but it had become known.

It lived in the space between them.

Kia felt it before she could organize it, before she could shape it into something reasonable, before she could even decide whether she was ready to let herself look at it directly.

It was there in the way her body no longer prepared itself when she approached him, in the way her breath settled instead of catching, in the way silence had stopped feeling like a gap to cross and had become something they could simply inhabit together.

They had found something new—not fragile, not uncertain, but different.

The afternoon stretched wide across Central Park, sunlight filtering through the trees in soft layers, warming the grass, the benches, the spaces where people sat inside their own lives without needing to explain them.

Somewhere beyond the paths, a child called out and was answered by another voice farther away. A dog pulled free just long enough to be chased laughing.

The city moved at a distance, present but not pressing, as if even it understood that something quieter was taking place here.

Ajah sat at the piano, not playing yet, his hands resting loosely on his thighs, posture relaxed in the way true ease was relaxed—not from the absence of tension, but from trust in the moment itself.

The piano sat angled into the light, its dark surface catching broken pieces of sun through the branches above. The bench beneath them held the faint warmth of the afternoon.

Kia sat beside him, closer than she had before, not touching, but not keeping distance either, and that difference was everything.

She leaned back slightly, her hands braced behind her on the bench, her face tilted toward the sky, eyes half-closed as she let the warmth settle into her skin.

The light moved across her cheekbones, through the dark fall of her hair, across her throat where her breath rose and fell more slowly than it once would have in the presence of something she could feel but hadn't yet named.

For a moment, she allowed herself to exist without thinking about how she appeared, how she sounded, how she was being received.

There was no audience here, no role to enter, no performance to deliver.

Just her.

Ajah turned his head slightly, watching her—not with curiosity, not with analysis, not even with surprise, but with recognition.

"You're quieter today."

Kia smiled without opening her eyes. *"I think I'm just not fighting anything."*

The answer settled between them, not heavy, not light—true.

Ajah nodded once, his gaze lingering for a moment before shifting forward again to the open stretch of park in front of them.

"That's a good place to be."

Kia lowered her chin slightly, opening her eyes, turning just enough to look at him.

"It's new," she admitted.

He met her gaze.

"New doesn't mean unfamiliar. Sometimes it just means you're finally letting yourself stay."

The words didn't pass through her quickly.

They settled. Kia studied him for a moment, something softer moving through her expression now, something less guarded, less measured, something that no longer needed the protection of distance to remain intact.

"You do that a lot."

Ajah raised an eyebrow slightly.

"Do what?"

She shifted her weight, turning toward him more fully now, posture open, attention fully engaged.

"You say things like that. Like you're not trying to impress me, but you're still... reaching something."

Ajah let out a quiet breath that almost resembled a laugh. His shoulders relaxed further, and something in his face softened in response to being seen that clearly.

"I'm not trying to reach anything. I'm just saying what feels true."

Kia held his gaze, her expression thoughtful, but warmer now, more direct.

"That's what I mean."

The moment stretched—not awkward, not uncertain, aware.

A breeze moved through the trees, lifting a strand of her hair across her face. The air carried a slight coolness beneath the warmth, enough to make skin newly conscious of itself.

Kia reached up instinctively to move the strand back.

Before her fingers could touch it, Ajah's hand lifted slightly—and stopped.

He did not touch her.

He paused there, just short of contact, as if the possibility itself had arrived first and both of them were required to acknowledge it before either could move beyond it.

Kia noticed, and in that pause, something changed. Not because he touched her—because he didn't—because the awareness of the possibility entered the space between them, quiet but undeniable, and neither of them rushed to erase it.

Kia lowered her hand slowly. Her breath shifted, just slightly, her chest rising a little deeper than before. She didn't move away. She didn't move closer either.

She stayed.

Ajah lowered his hand again, his fingers coming to rest lightly against the edge of the bench, posture still grounded, but something in his presence more aware now, more openly attentive to the charge that had entered the moment and chosen to remain.

"Can I ask you something?" Kia said after a beat.

Ajah nodded. *"Yeah."*

She held his gaze, voice steady, but softer now than it had been a minute before.

"Do you feel this?"

The question wasn't vague. It didn't need elaboration. Everything that had not been named between them suddenly stood there, fully visible, asking only whether it was shared.

Ajah didn't answer immediately, not because he didn't know, but because he understood what the answer would make real.

He exhaled slowly, his eyes remaining on hers.

"Yeah."

No elaboration. No softening. No deflection.

Just truth.

Kia nodded once, her lips pressing together briefly, not to hold anything back, but to keep the moment from spilling too quickly into something larger than it needed to become all at once.

"Okay."

And that was enough.

Neither of them rushed to define it. Neither of them reached for language that would try to fix in place something still unfolding of its own accord.

They didn't need to, because it was already there.

Ajah turned slightly back toward the piano.

His hands lifted and rested lightly on the keys, and for a second he stayed still, as if listening for where the moment wanted the music to begin.

Then he played.

The music didn't announce itself.

It emerged, soft, measured, but carrying something deeper now, something that had always existed under the surface and was only now being allowed into the air without disguise.

The notes moved with restraint, but not distance, with tenderness, but not hesitation.

It was not a performance of feeling. It was feeling.

Kia listened, her body relaxing into the sound, her mind no longer trying to analyze what was happening, no longer checking the moment for imbalance or danger or future consequence.

This time, the music didn't guide her. It met her.

She shifted slightly, and her shoulder brushed against his arm.

Not intentional. Not accidental. Just enough to register.

Ajah didn't move away.

Neither did she.

The contact remained, light, unforced, but present.

Kia closed her eyes again, breathing steady, her body no longer preparing itself for rupture, no longer trying to get ahead of what the closeness might mean.

She let herself feel it—not just the music, not just the moment—the closeness, the safety, the quiet, undeniable awareness that something real had taken root between them, something that did not demand naming, did not rush toward conclusion, did not need to be declared to exist with weight.

Ajah's playing softened near the end, the final notes stretching a little longer than usual, as if he was allowing the moment to land fully before letting it go.

When his hands finally lifted from the keys, the silence that followed did not feel empty.

It felt complete.

Kia opened her eyes slowly, turning her head just enough to look at him.

He was already looking at her, no hesitation, no uncertainty, just presence.

Kia smiled, small but certain.

"That answered my question."

Something warm settled into Ajah's expression.

"Good."

Neither of them moved right away. Neither of them broke the space they had just created.

Because for the first time, they were not standing on opposite sides of something unspoken.

They were inside it.

Together.

And it didn't feel overwhelming.

It felt right.

Chapter Twenty: The Past Didn't Knock This Time

The call came when Kia was not prepared to be pulled backward, which meant it came at the exact right moment.

She had just left Central Park, the softness of the afternoon still resting on her skin, the quiet steadiness of her time with Ajah lingering in her chest like something she had stopped questioning and begun to trust.

The city had thickened again around her—traffic building, voices rising, light shifting toward that restless hour when everyone seemed to be moving toward something at once—but Kia moved through it differently now.

She wasn't bracing, she wasn't scanning, she wasn't anticipating disruption before it arrived.

Her body had learned, at least in pieces, that not every transition carried danger, and that was why the vibration of her phone felt so sharp when it came.

Not because of the sound, but because of the contrast—because she had just been somewhere steady, somewhere shared, somewhere that had begun to feel like something she could remain inside of without preparing for it to break.

One pulse in her hand. Easy to ignore.

Almost easy enough that she might have.

She pulled it from her bag half-looking, still walking, still carrying the afterglow of the park in her body, and then she saw the name, and her breath changed before she answered.

Aunt Lian.

Kia stopped, not abruptly, but completely.

The city did not go quiet. Cars still moved through the avenue. Someone laughed too loudly a few steps away. A siren called from farther downtown, distant enough not to demand alarm but near enough to remind her that urgency always belonged to somebody, but all of it moved further away as she stared at the screen for a beat longer than she needed to, her thumb hovering just above the answer icon, her body already remembering things her mind had not yet allowed to surface.

Then she answered.

"Hello?"

There was a pause, not empty, heavy.

"Kia..."

Her aunt's voice came softer than she remembered, but carrying something underneath it that hadn't changed—a pressure, a caution, the tone of someone already living inside difficult information. Kia closed her eyes briefly, grounding, the echo of Ajah's presence still somewhere in her body, now colliding with something older.

"What's wrong?"

Because there was always something wrong.

Another pause, longer this time.

"It's your mother."

The words didn't land at first, not fully.

They hovered, waiting for shape, waiting for meaning. Kia didn't speak, couldn't yet.

"She had an episode," Aunt Lian continued, her voice tightening just slightly.

"It's worse this time."

Kia's fingers tightened around the phone, her jaw setting without permission.

"Worse how?"

Silence, then—

"She's asking for you."

That landed.

Kia exhaled slowly, but it didn't release anything. It pressed something deeper into her chest, something old and immediate and impossible to sort through standing on a sidewalk with strangers moving around her.

"Where is she?"

"St. Vincent's," Aunt Lian said. *"They admitted her this morning."*

The city came rushing back then—sound, movement, presence—but Kia no longer felt inside of it. She felt pulled.

"I'll be there."

She didn't ask anything else, didn't gather details, didn't let herself imagine too far ahead, because thinking would complicate something her body had already decided.

The hospital smelled like memory, not one memory, not one scene, but layered memory.

Kia stepped through the automatic doors and felt her shoulders tighten before she told them to, the shift immediate, her senses sharpening in ways she had not felt in years, every fluorescent light too bright, every polished floor too reflective, every distant voice too controlled in the way controlled spaces often were.

She hated places like this, not because of what they were, but because of what they represented—control, loss of it, the illusion of it.

Hospitals always carried that same contradiction: order imposed over unraveling, clipboards, monitors, low voices, people trying to speak in measured tones while bodies and minds did whatever they were going to do anyway.

Kia approached the front desk, her voice steady even as something inside her shifted.

"I'm here for Mei Lin Zhang."

The name felt formal in her mouth, distant, like something written on paperwork instead of something that had once called her in from another room, once corrected her posture, once laughed in the kitchen, once filled whole apartments with unpredictability.

The nurse glanced at the screen, then back at her.

"Family?"

Kia hesitated, just for a second.

"...Daughter."

The word felt heavier than it should have, like it carried more rooms than this one.

The hallway to her mother's room felt too long, not because of distance, but because each step gave memory time to catch up—the muted roll of a cart somewhere behind her, the smell of disinfectant mixed with something metallic and stale, the steady beeping from rooms she didn't pass closely enough to see into, the air-conditioning too cool against skin that already felt alert.

By the time she reached the doorway, her body had gone fully still inside itself.

The room was too quiet, not peaceful, controlled.

Kia stood there for a moment before stepping inside, her body slowing as if it needed to measure each movement carefully before allowing the next.

Her mother looked smaller.

That was the first thing she noticed, not fragile, but reduced.

Mei Lin sat upright in the hospital bed, her frame slight beneath the pale gown, hair unbrushed and falling loosely around her face in uneven strands, her skin thinner somehow, not weaker, more exposed, but her eyes—still sharp, still alert, still capable of turning a room the moment they fixed on someone.

They shifted the instant Kia entered, and in that instant everything that had ever existed between them returned—recognition, tension, love, fear, all at once.

"You came."

Her mother's voice was soft, too soft.

Kia stepped further in, hands at her sides, posture controlled, breath measured.

"They said you asked for me."

Mei Lin's lips curved slightly, not quite a smile, not quite something else.

"You don't visit unless I ask."

The words were not accusatory. They didn't need to be.

Kia didn't answer that.

She moved closer instead, stopping just short of the bed, her eyes taking in details she did not want to study too closely—the hospital bracelet, the blanket folded too sharply over her mother's lap, the cup of water untouched on the side table, a plastic bag of personal belongings tied closed and set in the chair by the wall.

"What happened?"

Mei Lin tilted her head slightly, her gaze sharpening.

"You always want explanations. Like things make sense when you name them."

Kia's jaw tightened.

"Sometimes they do."

A beat, then Mei Lin laughed. It wasn't loud, it wasn't wild, but it wasn't steady either.

"You sound like your father."

That shifted something.

Kia felt it in her chest immediately, the mention of him not as comfort, not yet, but as a pressure point that still knew exactly where to live inside her.

"How is he?"

The question came before she could stop it.

Mei Lin's expression changed, subtly but unmistakably.

"Still calm. Still pretending everything can be held together if he just... stays quiet enough."

Kia looked down briefly, her breath catching before steadying again.

"He did more than stay quiet."

Mei Lin's eyes flickered.

"Did he?"

The question wasn't curiosity. It was challenge.

Kia lifted her gaze again, her posture firmer now, something inside her no longer willing to shrink under it.

"He stayed."

The room shifted, not visibly, but in temperature, in gravity.

Mei Lin didn't respond immediately.

Her eyes moved over Kia's face, studying her in a way that felt both familiar and estranging at once, as if she were trying to find not who Kia was, but what version of her had arrived.

"And you?" she asked.

Kia blinked.

"What about me?"

Mei Lin's gaze didn't waver.

"Did you stay?"

The question landed deeper than Kia expected, because the answer wasn't simple.

She had stayed, but she had also left—emotionally, mentally, protectively, inwardly, in all the ways a child learns to leave a room while still standing in it.

Kia exhaled slowly, her shoulders lowering just slightly.

"I survived."

Mei Lin watched her for a long moment, then nodded, not agreement, recognition.

"That's not the same thing," she said quietly.

Kia felt something tighten in her chest again, but this time it did not rise into anger. It settled somewhere else—truth, because that was the part no one had ever said that cleanly before.

Survival had been movement, instinct, containment, but it had not been presence. It had not been staying.

The quiet in the room changed after that, not easier, more honest. The monitor at her mother's bedside kept its rhythm. The fluorescent lights remained relentless.

Somewhere outside the door, shoes moved across the hallway in brisk, practiced steps, but inside the room, something had been named that could not be unnamed again.

Hours later, Kia stepped back out into the city, and the air hit her differently now—cooler, thinner.

Her body carried something heavier than it had when she walked in, not just the hospital, not just her mother, the sentence too—*That's not the same thing.*

It stayed in her, pressing against everything she thought she understood about endurance and love and the cost of both. And beneath that weight, something else moved—quieter, but present—the memory of the afternoon, of stillness, of music, of a space where she had not needed to defend herself against what she felt.

Her phone vibrated again.

Ajah.

She stared at the screen longer this time, then answered.

"Hey."

His voice came through immediately, steady, familiar.

"You okay?"

The question landed differently now. Kia looked out at the street, her eyes unfocused, her mind still partially inside that room, that chair, that question, that version of her mother who had looked reduced and yet somehow more exact.

"I don't know yet."

There was no pause on his end, no hesitation.

"Where are you?"

Kia exhaled slowly.

"Outside St. Vincent's."

A beat, then—

"Stay there. I'm coming."

Kia closed her eyes briefly. For a moment, she almost said no, almost told him she could handle it, almost reached for the version of herself that carried everything alone because carrying it alone felt more familiar than being met while still shaken.

But this time—she didn't.

"...Okay."

And for the first time, letting someone come toward her didn't feel like weakness.

It felt like choice.

And somewhere between the past that still held weight and the present that was asking her to trust something new, Kia stood still, waiting, not for rescue, but for connection.

Chapter Twenty-One: What Stayed When She Didn't Run

Kia didn't move from the spot where she had stopped. The city refused to acknowledge her stillness.

Taxis edged forward in impatient inches, engines humming low like something restrained.

Pedestrians slipped around one another with practiced precision, shoulders brushing, eyes forward, momentum uninterrupted.

A burst of laughter rose somewhere behind her, sharp and brief, dissolving into the steady rhythm of footsteps against concrete.

Life continued—loud, uninterrupted—and still she stood there, not frozen, not stuck, but suspended in something that had not finished moving through her yet.

She had said *okay*, and the word had stayed with her, not as surrender, not as dependence, but as choice, and now she stood inside the space that choice had opened.

The hospital doors opened and closed behind her in quiet mechanical intervals, releasing fragments of other people's lives into the air—voices low, footsteps slower, breaths heavier than when they entered.

A woman wiped her eyes as she passed. A man adjusted his coat without looking up. A nurse laughed too loudly at something that wasn't funny.

Pieces of impact moved around her, but none of them landed on Kia fully, because part of her had not left.

Her mother's voice did not echo. It pressed, low and steady.

Did you stay? Kia inhaled, but the breath didn't settle where it should. It hovered high in her chest, incomplete, like something interrupted before it could finish becoming.

The question didn't leave her. It anchored somewhere beneath her ribs, where answers don't organize themselves cleanly. Because the truth didn't line up.

She had stayed in ways that hollowed her, left in ways that rebuilt her, and now, standing in the narrow space between both, she couldn't tell which one her mother had meant.

And beneath that, quieter but just as present, was the memory of the afternoon—of stillness, of music, of a space where she had not needed to defend herself against what she felt.

Both lived in her now, not canceling each other out, but pressing in from different directions.

A car door shut closer this time. Footsteps followed—measured, unhurried, the kind that didn't need to rush to arrive.

Kia felt it before she turned, not anticipation, not relief, recognition.

Ajah stopped a few feet away, not stepping into her space immediately, not calling her name again, just arriving.

His eyes moved over her face, not searching for damage, not scanning for explanation, just registering what was there without trying to change it.

"Hey."

The word came quiet enough that it didn't compete with the city.

Kia turned then, her expression holding, but only just.

"Hey."

The word sat between them, thin, stretched slightly at the edges.

Ajah stepped closer, not closing the distance completely, just enough that the space between them no longer felt necessary.

He didn't ask what happened, didn't reach for the version of her that explained things.

He waited.

Kia held his gaze longer than she meant to, something tightening in her chest—not resistance, not fear, something closer to exposure.

"She asked for me."

Her voice didn't crack, but it didn't protect her either.

Ajah nodded once. *"Okay."*

No weight added. No meaning assigned. Just room.

Kia looked away, her gaze drifting toward the movement of traffic, her fingers brushing against each other as if trying to release something that didn't have a clear direction.

"It was the same... and it wasn't."

A bus hissed to a stop nearby, doors folding open, people stepping down without looking at her, without knowing anything about the moment she was standing inside.

Ajah didn't interrupt.

"She looked smaller," Kia continued, her brow tightening as the image returned, not visually, but physically, settling somewhere behind her sternum.

"But her voice..." Her breath caught, just briefly. *"...it still knew exactly where to land."*

That lingered longer than she expected.

"She asked me if I stayed."

Ajah's presence shifted—not visibly, but in depth, something steadier.

"What did you say?"

Kia let out a breath that didn't fully release.

"I said I survived."

A pause stretched between them as the city pressed forward.

"She said that wasn't the same thing."

Silence didn't fall. It thickened.

Ajah stepped closer this time, intentionally.

"How did that feel?"

Kia let out something that almost passed for a laugh, but it didn't carry through.

"Like she was right."

No defense. No cushioning. Just placement.

Ajah watched her, not softening it, not correcting it.

"Do you think she was?"

Kia didn't answer immediately, because the answer shifted depending on where she stood inside it. Her shoulders lifted slightly with her breath, then dropped.

"I think..." she started, quieter now, the words moving slower, like they had weight this time.

"I think I stayed as much as I could without breaking."

Her fingers pressed together, grounding.

"...and then I left the parts that were breaking me."

The air shifted, not outside, inside her.

Ajah nodded, not approving, not reframing, accepting.

"That sounds like staying to me."

Kia looked at him, something tightening at the edge of her eyes.

"It doesn't feel like it."

Ajah moved closer again, now within reach.

"That's because you learned to measure staying by endurance, not by what it cost you."

This time the words didn't land in her head. They landed in her body, somewhere deeper, somewhere older.

"She's still in there," Kia said, her voice quieter now. *"And I walked out."*

"You didn't walk out," Ajah said. *"You stepped away so you could breathe."*

Her chest tightened, and then something inside it shifted, subtle but undeniable.

"It doesn't feel like breathing."

Ajah didn't look away.

"That's because you just came out of holding it in."

That did it.

Her shoulders dropped, not controlled, not intentional, released. Her eyes filled, not dramatically, not collapsing, just enough that she couldn't pretend she was unaffected anymore.

Ajah didn't reach for her right away. He stayed where he was, letting the moment exist without trying to manage it.

And when Kia's hand lifted, small, uncertain, he met it.

Not pulling her in. Not anchoring her down.

Just holding.

The contact was light, but it traveled through her fingers, up her arm, into her chest, where everything had been held too tightly for too long.

Her breath came uneven at first, then deeper, then fuller.

This time she didn't correct it, didn't reshape it, didn't contain it.

She let it move.

Ajah's thumb shifted slightly against the back of her hand, not soothing, not distracting, just reminding.

You're not alone in this.

The city didn't stop, didn't quiet, didn't soften, but between them something did.

When Kia finally looked at him again, her eyes clearer, her body steadier, something had shifted in the way she occupied herself—more present, less guarded.

"I didn't want to call you."

Ajah's brow lifted slightly.

"Why not?"

"Because I didn't want this to be the reason you were here."

That sat differently.

"I'm here because you called."

Kia shook her head slightly.

"You said you were coming."

A small shift in his mouth, not quite a smile.

"And you said okay."

That landed.

Kia exhaled, something loosening.

"...yeah."

They stood there, not figuring it out, not defining it, just inside it.

And for the first time, Kia understood something she had never allowed herself to fully name.

Love was not what showed up when things were easy.

It was what stayed when things weren't.

Her fingers tightened slightly around his, not clinging, not asking, acknowledging.

Ajah didn't move away.

He stayed.

And this time—so did she.

Chapter Twenty-Two: The Man Who Stayed

The hallway outside her father's apartment still smelled the same—not identical, not preserved in time, but familiar in the way certain old places remained familiar even after years had layered themselves over them, cooking oil long absorbed into walls, old wood, detergent, a trace of something metallic from pipes that had seen too much life and kept going anyway.

The scent settled into her chest before she had even fully decided how to feel about it.

Kia stood in front of the door longer than she needed to, not because she didn't want to go in, but because she knew that once she did, she would not simply be stepping into an apartment.

She would be stepping into a version of herself she had spent years learning how to outgrow—the girl who listened before she spoke, the girl who knew how to read tension from the way footsteps sounded through a room, the girl who had learned to survive by becoming observant, careful, useful, quiet when needed, emotionally absent when necessary, present only in pieces.

And still, beneath that awareness, something steadier remained—the understanding she had just begun to accept outside the hospital, that staying did not have to look the same to be real, that what she was learning now did not erase where she had come from, but stood beside it.

Ajah stood beside her, not touching her, not crowding her, but close enough that she could feel his presence without turning her head, grounded, patient.

His stillness did not ask anything from her.

It didn't urge her forward or try to soften what the doorway meant.

It simply stayed available, the same way he had outside St. Vincent's, not filling space, just holding it.

"You don't have to rush this," he said quietly.

Kia nodded once, her hand lifting toward the door, then pausing just before her knuckles made contact.

"I'm not rushing."

And she wasn't. Her body was alert, yes.

Her breath was shallower than usual. But none of it felt like panic. It felt like knowing.

She knocked.

The sound echoed differently than it used to, not louder, not softer, heavier, like time had thickened around wood and walls and memory, changing the way things traveled without changing what they were made of.

Footsteps moved on the other side, slow, measured, familiar in a way that pulled something deep from her memory before she had time to brace against it.

Then the door opened.

Her father stood there.

Time had not taken him, but it had marked him.

He was still tall, his six-foot-three frame filling the doorway with the same quiet authority she remembered, shoulders broad, posture steady, presence grounded in a way that had never needed explanation.

His skin still held that deep, warm brown that seemed to absorb light rather than reflect it. His hands were still the hands of a working man, large and capable, marked by years of doing, repairing, building, carrying.

But time had left its record. New lines had settled around his eyes, into the space between his brows, into the corners of his mouth where silence had apparently rested longer than it used to.

His face did not look tired exactly. It looked used—used by responsibility, used by commitment, used by the long practice of staying.

He looked at her, not surprised, not confused. He had been expecting her.

"Kia."

Her name in his voice had not changed.

Something moved through her chest then, something both steady and fragile at once, something that had always existed beneath everything else and rarely needed to be named because it had always been there.

"Hey, Daddy."

The word came easier than she expected. It didn't catch, didn't embarrass her with sentiment. It simply arrived.

He stepped back immediately, opening the door wider.

"Come in."

No hesitation. No conditions. Just space.

Kia stepped inside.

The apartment hadn't changed much, or maybe it had changed in ways that were harder to see.

The furniture sat mostly where it had always been, the couch still slightly worn at the arms, the table still carrying the quiet weight of meals that had once been eaten in silence or in conversations careful enough not to disturb something unstable.

The curtains hung the same way, a little uneven at one side. The lamp in the corner still cast the same yellowed light that made evening feel contained instead of open.

The room felt lived in, not heavy, not stale, but layered with a history that had not been cleared away, only arranged so it could keep being survived.

Ajah followed her in, his presence quiet but aware, his eyes taking in the space without intruding on it.

Her father closed the door behind them, his gaze shifting briefly to Ajah, assessing, not suspicious, not guarded, attentive.

"This him?"

Kia turned slightly, her body angling between them, not as barrier, but as bridge.

"This is Ajah."

Ajah stepped forward just enough, his posture respectful, his presence steady.

"Mr. Harris."

Her father's eyes lingered on him for a moment longer, weighing what mattered and discarding what didn't. Then he nodded once.

"Call me James."

The simplicity of it carried more weight than politeness alone, acceptance not complete, not assumed, but open.

Ajah nodded. *"James."*

The exchange settled something in the room, and Kia felt it immediately, the tension in her shoulders lowering just slightly.

"How is she?"

Her father's gaze shifted back to her. His expression tightened, not dramatically, not outwardly emotional, but in a way she recognized at once—containment, that old, practiced containment that had never meant emptiness, only control over what could be controlled.

"Stable," he said.

The word didn't reassure her. It never had. Stability in their family had always been conditional, provisional, capable of changing shape before anyone finished trusting it.

"That doesn't tell me anything."

James nodded once, as if acknowledging the truth of that without needing to defend the word he'd chosen.

"It means she's not a danger to herself right now," he said. *"And they're adjusting her medication."*

Kia crossed her arms loosely, not defensive, holding herself.

"And after that?"

James looked at her for a long moment, his eyes steady, his posture unchanged.

"After that, we see."

Kia let out a quiet breath, something between frustration and understanding settling into her chest.

"That's what it's always been."

James didn't argue.

"That's what it's always been," he agreed.

The honesty of it didn't soften the moment, but it grounded it.

Kia looked away briefly, her gaze moving through the room, landing on details she might once have ignored but couldn't now—the tools in the corner, his work boots near the door, a folded receipt on the table, a mug with a chip at the rim, the remote placed square against the edge of the table as if even small things deserved order.

Proof of a man who had kept things running even when everything else hadn't.

And now, standing here after leaving the hospital, after choosing not to carry everything alone, she could see it differently—not as silence, not as absence, but as structure, as something that had held even when it couldn't fix.

"She asked if I stayed."

The words entered the room without preparation, as if the apartment itself had made room for them before she knew she was going to say them.

James's expression shifted, not outwardly, but inwardly, and Kia saw it.

"And what did you tell her?" he asked.

Kia turned back to him, her eyes steady now, her voice clearer than it had been outside the hospital.

"I told her I survived."

A pause.

"She said that wasn't the same thing."

The room held the weight of that. The apartment seemed to narrow around it, not claustrophobic, but focused.

Even the hum of the refrigerator in the kitchen seemed suddenly more noticeable, as if ordinary sounds had stepped back to let the words stand unchallenged.

James inhaled slowly, his chest rising, then falling in a controlled release.

"She's not wrong," he said.

Kia's brow tightened.

"You too?"

James shook his head.

"Not the way she meant it."

Kia waited, because with her father, there was always more.

He stepped closer, not imposing, not overwhelming, just present.

"Surviving is what you had to do," he said. *"Staying... that's what I chose to do."*

The words landed differently. Kia felt it, not as correction, but as separation, a line drawn not to diminish her, but to free her from comparison she had been carrying without realizing it.

"Why?" she asked.

The question wasn't new, but it had never been asked like this before, not from accusation, from wanting to understand the architecture of the man in front of her.

James held her gaze.

"Because I made a commitment," he said. *"To her. To you."*

Kia's jaw tightened slightly.

"Even when it was like that?"

James didn't look away.

"Especially when it was like that."

Silence settled into the room again.

Kia felt something shift inside her, not resistance, not rejection, but recognition of something she had never fully allowed herself to see clearly.

His staying had not been passive. It hadn't been standing there and absorbing damage because he didn't know what else to do. It had been active, deliberate, costly, a choice made again and again in rooms that gave him every reason to walk out and every responsibility not to.

And still—

he had done it.

Ajah stood quietly through all of it, his presence still, his eyes moving between them, not intruding, not silent out of discomfort, but understanding that this was not his moment to shape, only to witness.

Kia glanced at him briefly, then back at her father.

"That kind of staying..." she said slowly, *"...it's not the same as what I did."*

James nodded.

"It's not supposed to be."

Kia's breath caught slightly.

"Then what is it supposed to be?"

For the first time since she'd entered, something in James's face softened, not weak, not uncertain, but open in a way she had not often seen when she was young.

"Yours," he said.

The word landed, not heavy, not light, true.

Kia felt something loosen in her chest then, something she had held tight for years without quite knowing she was holding it, because for the first time she wasn't being measured against him, she wasn't being told endurance was the only respectable form of love, she wasn't being asked to prove her worth by matching his sacrifice.

She was being allowed to define herself.

Ajah shifted slightly beside her, his hand brushing gently against hers, not to interrupt, not to redirect, just to remind her that she wasn't standing alone in the middle of this understanding.

Kia didn't pull away.

She didn't cling either.

She let the contact exist.

James noticed. Of course he did. His gaze moved briefly to their hands, then back to Kia's face.

"You good?"

The question was simple, but it carried everything—how are you standing, what are you learning, do you know yourself in this moment, can you feel what's changing in you without running from it.

Kia inhaled slowly, her shoulders settling, her posture grounding.

She looked at him, then at Ajah, then back again.

"...I think I'm learning how to be."

James nodded once.

"That's all any of us doing," he said.

And in that moment, standing between the man who had shown her what staying looked like and the man who was showing her what choosing looked like, Kia understood something she had never been able to name cleanly before.

Love was not one thing.

It was not just endurance.

It was not just presence.

It was not just choice.

It was all of it.

And for the first time—she wasn't trying to separate them.

She was learning how to hold them both.

Chapter Twenty-Three: What Love Could Not Excuse

The hospital room felt smaller the second time, not because anything had changed, but because Kia had.

She didn't hesitate at the door this time, didn't pause to prepare herself, didn't brace in the same way she had before as if the room itself might shift shape depending on what waited inside it.

But her body still remembered—the scent of antiseptic, the faint metallic trace beneath it, the hum of machines, the stillness that wasn't peace but control, structured, monitored, contained, a quiet imposed over instability.

Kia stepped inside slowly, and her eyes found her mother immediately, as if there had never been any distance between them at all.

And beneath that movement was something newly steady, something shaped in the space she had just come from—the understanding that staying, choosing, and surviving did not cancel each other out, but existed alongside one another, and that she no longer had to shrink to make sense of any of it.

Mei Lin Zhang sat upright again, but differently this time, not diminished, not softened, present.

Her hair had been brushed and pulled back loosely now, revealing the architecture of her face more clearly—the defined cheekbones, the narrow jaw, the eyes that had always carried too much awareness for their own good.

Her skin, pale with that faint undertone of gold, held a quiet fragility that might have made someone unfamiliar with her mistake delicacy for helplessness.

Kia knew better. There had never been anything helpless about her mother.

Mei Lin looked up the moment Kia entered, her gaze locking onto her daughter with a focus that felt immediate and intentional, as if the hours between visits had not blurred anything at all.

"You came back."

Kia moved further into the room, her steps steady, her posture grounded in a way that was new even to herself.

"I said I would."

The words held, no tension, no performance, just truth.

Mei Lin studied her longer than necessary, her head tilting slightly, her eyes narrowing, not with suspicion, but assessment.

It was a look Kia knew well, one that had once made her feel small because it always seemed to suggest she was being measured against something she could not see.

"You look different."

Kia didn't look away.

"I am."

The simplicity of it landed heavier than any explanation could have.

Mei Lin's lips curved slightly, not quite a smile, not quite something else.

"People always think they change," she said. *"Until they're tested."*

The words moved through Kia, but they didn't destabilize her the way they once would have.

Years ago, a sentence like that might have rearranged her from the inside, sending her instantly into interpretation, defense, adjustment. Now it arrived, touched something, and stopped there.

"I've been tested."

Mei Lin's gaze sharpened.

"Not like this."

The air shifted.

Kia stepped closer, stopping beside the bed this time, not at a distance, not guarded, but not leaning in either, balanced.

"Then let's not pretend."

The words came softer than confrontation, but firmer than avoidance.

Mei Lin's eyes flickered.

"About what?"

Kia exhaled slowly, her hands resting at her sides, her fingers still but no longer clenched.

"About what it was like."

Silence filled the room, not empty, full. Mei Lin leaned back slightly, her expression shifting, not defensive, not dismissive, but aware.

The hospital pillow behind her rustled faintly. A machine somewhere to the left blinked and hummed in indifferent rhythm. Outside the door, a cart rolled past and kept going. Inside the room, nothing moved except the truth.

"You remember too much."

Kia shook her head once.

"I remember enough."

The distinction mattered. It wasn't a claim to perfect memory. It was a refusal to let uncertainty be used as an eraser.

Mei Lin watched her, her posture still, her gaze steady.

"Then say it."

The invitation wasn't gentle. It wasn't warm. It was direct, and somehow that made it cleaner.

Kia felt it then, every memory pressing forward at once, not scattered now, not arriving in flashes or emotional fragments, aligned, ready.

Her breath steadied.

"You were unpredictable."

The word landed without accusation, without softness, truth.

Mei Lin didn't flinch.

Kia continued.

"Not just moody. Not just emotional. You shifted without warning. One moment you were laughing, the next you were screaming. One moment you were holding me, the next you were pushing me away like I was the reason something inside you hurt."

Her voice didn't rise. It deepened.

"I didn't know which version of you I was coming home to. And that..."

She paused, her breath catching just slightly before continuing. *"...that changes a child."*

The room held the weight of her words.

Mei Lin's expression didn't collapse. It didn't harden. It stilled.

"You think I didn't know that?" she asked quietly.

Kia blinked, not because the question confused her, but because it opened a door she hadn't expected.

"I knew," Mei Lin continued, her voice lower now, steadier in a way that felt chosen.

"I saw it in your face. In the way you watched me instead of coming to me. In the way you stood near the door like you were ready to leave before anything even happened."

Kia's chest tightened. There was something unbearable in being seen that accurately by the person who had helped create the need to live that way in the first place.

"Then why didn't you stop?"

The question came without softness, without cushioning. It had waited too long.

Mei Lin inhaled slowly, her shoulders lifting just slightly before settling again.

"Because I didn't know how."

The answer didn't explode, didn't unravel. It sat, plain.

Kia felt it, not as relief, not as justification, as something else, a limit, a truth that could be understood without making anything easier.

And in that moment, she could feel the difference between her father's staying, Ajah's choosing, and her mother's inability to hold either consistently—not as judgment, but as clarity.

"You didn't try."

Mei Lin's eyes sharpened again.

"I did."

Kia shook her head.

"Not in a way that I could feel."

That landed.

Mei Lin looked at her for a long moment, her gaze no longer sharp, no longer guarded, just present.

"That's fair."

The words shifted the room. Kia hadn't prepared for them, hadn't braced against them, and because of that, they reached her, but they didn't undo anything.

"Fair doesn't fix it."

Mei Lin nodded.

"No. It doesn't."

Silence settled again.

Kia felt something rise then, not anger, not pain alone, but something deeper, something that had been forming beneath everything else while she stood there trying not to let the room control her breathing.

"Do you know what I learned from you?"

Mei Lin tilted her head slightly.

"What?"

Kia exhaled slowly.

"I learned how to leave a room without moving."

The words landed hard because they were exact.

"I learned how to disappear while standing right in front of someone. How to become whatever was safest in the moment instead of who I actually was."

Her voice didn't shake.

"That's not just survival. That's... losing yourself before you even know who you are."

Mei Lin's expression changed then, not dramatically, but deeply, as if something inside her had shifted place.

"And you think that's all I gave you?"

Kia paused, because the answer was no.

That was the complication she had carried for years. Hurt would have been easier if it had come from someone empty, if there had been nothing else to account for, if all she had inherited was damage, but that wasn't true, and truth, if it was going to matter here, had to remain whole.

"...No."

Mei Lin watched her carefully.

"Then say that too."

Kia inhaled slowly, her chest rising, her thoughts aligning.

"You gave me awareness," she said. *"You made me pay attention. You made me read people, read rooms, feel things most people don't notice."*

Her voice softened slightly. *"You gave me depth."*

Mei Lin's gaze didn't waver.

"And pain."

The balance settled, truth without distortion, no glorifying, no erasing, no splitting her mother into saint or wound.

Mei Lin nodded slowly, her shoulders lowering just slightly.

"That's the part people don't like to admit," she said. *"That both can exist."*

Kia met her gaze.

"I'm not people."

A pause, then Mei Lin smiled, small, real.

"No," she said. *"You're not."*

The moment held, not resolved, not healed, but honest.

Kia stepped back slightly, not retreating, just shifting her space, allowing breath to move more freely through her body now that the room no longer required as much guarding.

"I don't know if I can forgive everything."

The admission didn't fracture the room. It grounded it.

Mei Lin nodded once.

"You don't have to."

Kia's brow tightened slightly.

"Then what am I supposed to do with it?"

Mei Lin looked at her, her gaze softer now, but still clear.

"Carry what's yours," she said. *"And leave what isn't."*

The words didn't feel easy, but they felt possible, possible in the way difficult truths sometimes did when they finally arrived clean enough not to require immediate agreement.

Kia exhaled slowly, her shoulders lowering, her body no longer bracing against the next impact.

She wasn't finished, not with this, not with her, not with the years that still lived underneath certain tones of voice and sudden changes in light and the smell of hospital air and the memory of waiting near doorways, but for the first time, she wasn't trapped inside it either.

And somewhere between truth that didn't soften and love that didn't excuse, Kia stood, not as a child trying to survive, but as a woman learning how to hold the weight without letting it define her.

Chapter Twenty-Four: What She Chose to Carry, What She Chose to Lay Down

Kia did not leave the hospital immediately, and that in itself was new.

In the past, moments like this—heavy, layered, emotionally charged—had required distance to survive.

Her body would have moved before her mind caught up. She would have stepped outside, inhaled sharply, and walked without direction until the feeling thinned enough to be manageable, until it became something she could fold, store, and revisit only when she had the strength to contain it again.

But this time she didn't rush to escape it.

The urge was there, faint, recognizable, but it no longer controlled her movement, so she stayed.

Not because the moment was easy, but because she was no longer trying to outrun what it held.

She had already faced it, named it, and something inside her had shifted enough to allow her to remain.

She sat, not in the chair beside her mother's bed, not close enough to be pulled back into the version of herself that had once lived in reaction, in anticipation, in constant emotional recalibration, but not at the doorway either, not halfway turned, not ready to leave.

In the middle.

A place she had never occupied before, a place that did not exist when she was younger because survival had required edges—either closeness or distance, presence or disappearance, engagement or retreat.

The middle required something else: stability, ownership, choice.

Mei Lin watched her without speaking, her eyes steady, her posture no longer performing strength or fragility, no longer arranging itself to control perception or deflect interpretation.

She simply existed, and that felt unfamiliar, almost unguarded. The silence between them did not demand to be filled. It allowed something to unfold.

Kia leaned forward slightly, her forearms resting on her thighs, her hands loosely clasped, fingers touching but not gripping, her gaze lowered not in avoidance, but in thought. She felt her breath, not shallow, not forced, present.

"I used to pray for you to change," she said quietly.

The words came without tension, without expectation. They didn't reach toward her mother to land. They came from her and settled where they needed to.

Mei Lin did not respond immediately.

Kia continued.

"Not in a big way. Not like... completely different. Just... enough that I could predict you. Enough that I could come home and not feel like I needed to prepare myself first."

Her voice softened, not from fragility, but from clarity.

"I thought if I was good enough, calm enough, quiet enough... it might make it easier for you to stay that way."

She lifted her gaze then, meeting her mother's eyes directly, no flinch, no softening of the truth.

"It didn't."

Mei Lin inhaled slowly, her chest rising, her fingers shifting slightly against the blanket, a small movement, but Kia noticed it now in a way she wouldn't have before, not as a signal to react, just as information.

"No," she said.

Not defensive. Not dismissive. Just true.

Kia nodded once, her expression steady, her breath even.

"I carried that for a long time," she said.

"Thinking I had some part in how you moved... how you shifted."

She paused, not because she was unsure, but because she was placing the truth exactly where it belonged.

"I don't carry that anymore."

The words didn't rise. They settled, and something in her body followed them, a release she could feel, not dramatic, not overwhelming, but precise.

Mei Lin's eyes searched her face, something deeper moving behind them now, less controlled, less defined, less practiced.

"That's good," she said quietly.

Kia studied her, not as a child looking for confirmation, but as a woman recognizing alignment.

"It doesn't mean I don't feel it sometimes," she added. *"It just means I don't believe it."*

The distinction held weight. Feeling was no longer authority. Belief was now chosen.

Mei Lin nodded slowly, her shoulders lowering just slightly.

The room shifted, not because anything had been resolved, but because something had been released.

Kia leaned back in her chair, her spine meeting it fully this time, her body no longer hovering in readiness.

Her hands opened slightly in her lap, her palms resting upward, her fingers no longer holding onto anything that required containment. For a moment, neither of them spoke.

Then—

"Do you still pray?" Mei Lin asked.

The question entered the space differently than the others, not sharp, not testing, curious.

Kia blinked, her brow tightening slightly, not from confusion, but from the unexpected direction of the conversation.

"...Yes."

Mei Lin's head tilted slightly.

"For me?"

Kia exhaled softly, feeling the question land not as pressure, but as something that required precision.

"Not the way I used to," she said.

Mei Lin waited, and this time Kia didn't rush to fill the space. She chose her words.

"I don't pray for you to change anymore," she explained. *"I pray for understanding. For peace. For... space to exist without carrying everything at once."*

Her voice softened further, not because she was retreating, but because what she was saying no longer needed force.

"And sometimes… I pray for you to have that too."

Mei Lin's expression shifted again, not softened, opened, as if something inside her had been given permission to exist without needing to be defended or explained.

"You always had a way of finding something steady," she said.

Kia let out a small breath.

"I had to."

A beat.

"I didn't," Mei Lin said.

The admission landed quietly, but it carried weight, not as apology, not as absolution, as truth.

Kia felt it, not as something that erased what had been, but as something that filled in a space that had always existed without language.

She nodded once.

"I know."

The words didn't close anything, but they bridged something.

Later, outside the hospital, the air felt different, not lighter, but clearer.

The city still moved the same way, cars passing, people navigating around each other without acknowledgment, distant sirens threading through the background, but none of it pressed against her the way it had earlier.

Kia stepped onto the sidewalk slowly. Her body no longer carried the same tightness. Her breath moved deeper, more grounded, more her own.

Ajah stood where she had left him earlier, leaning slightly against the edge of a parked car.

His posture was relaxed, but not disengaged.

His presence remained attentive without being fixed.

His gaze lifted the moment he saw her.

He didn't move toward her immediately.

He waited.

Not because he was unsure, but because he understood that she needed to arrive as herself.

Kia walked toward him, her steps steady, her presence settled in a way that hadn't existed before she walked into that room.

When she reached him, she stopped close enough to feel his presence without needing to reach for it.

"How was it?"

Kia let out a slow breath, her shoulders lowering slightly.

"Different."

Ajah studied her, not searching for cracks, not scanning for damage, but recognizing the shift.

"You look different."

Kia smiled faintly.

"She said that too."

A small pause.

"I didn't forgive everything."

Ajah nodded.

"You don't have to."

Kia looked at him, her expression steady.

"I know," she said. *"But I let some things go."*

The words held, and this time they didn't feel like an attempt. They felt like a decision already made.

Ajah stepped closer then, not abruptly, not hesitantly, just enough to close the space that no longer needed to exist.

"That's a start."

Kia nodded.

"It feels like one."

The moment settled between them, not dramatic, not overwhelming, grounded.

Ajah's hand lifted slowly, resting lightly against her arm, not pulling, not guiding, just there.

Kia didn't pull away. She didn't brace.

She allowed it.

And in that small, quiet contact, something stabilized, not because everything was resolved, but because she was no longer navigating it alone.

Kia looked at him for a moment longer, her eyes steady, her voice soft but certain.

"I used to think love meant holding everything together."

Ajah listened, fully.

"Now?"

Kia exhaled slowly, and as she did, she felt the truth settle not just in her mind, but in her body.

"Now I think it means knowing what to hold... and what to release."

The truth didn't need validation, but Ajah gave it acknowledgment anyway.

"That sounds right."

Kia smiled faintly, not wide, not performative, real.

And as they stood there, the city moving, life continuing, the past still present but no longer consuming, Kia felt something she had never allowed herself to fully feel before, not relief, not closure, something quieter, something stronger.

Peace, not as the absence of pain, but as the ability to stand within it without losing herself.

And beside her, Ajah remained, not as something she needed, but as someone she chose.

Chapter Twenty-Five: Where All the Pieces Learned to Stand Together

The apartment felt different the next time Kia walked into it, not because anything inside had changed, but because she had stopped entering it as someone bracing for impact.

The shift was immediate, subtle, but undeniable, carrying forward from the clarity she had stepped into outside the hospital, from the quiet decision she had already made about what she would carry and what she would release.

The same worn couch greeted her, its fabric softened by years of use, its edges slightly faded where hands had rested, where weight had settled, where presence had lingered without announcement.

The same table stood in its place, carrying the quiet evidence of her father's routines—mail sorted into careful stacks, tools set aside with intention, a life maintained not for appearance, but for function.

The same light filtered through the window, but this time she noticed how it landed, how it caught the edges of objects, how it revealed instead of simply illuminating, how nothing in the room asked to be seen, but everything had been held.

Kia stepped further inside, not cautiously, not scanning, just entering, and for the first time, the space did not feel like something she needed to interpret before she could exist inside it.

It met her as she was, not as a place where things had been held together out of necessity, but as a place where someone had chosen to keep holding them, the same quiet steadiness she had begun to recognize, not just in him, but in herself.

Her father stood near the sink, his back partially turned, his hands moving with the same steady rhythm she had known her entire life.

There was no excess in his movement, no wasted motion. Each action followed the next with quiet certainty, as if time itself had learned to move in alignment with him.

He didn't rush, didn't fidget, didn't fill silence unnecessarily. He simply moved.

"You ate?" he asked without turning.

Kia smiled faintly, the expression arriving without effort, grounded in a place that no longer needed to prepare before responding.

"Not yet."

He nodded once, still facing the counter.

"Sit down. I'll fix something."

The offer wasn't new, but it landed differently. Before, it might have felt like routine or obligation. Now it felt like care expressed in the only language he had ever fully trusted, a language she no longer tried to translate into something else.

Kia moved to the table, pulling out a chair slowly, lowering herself into it without the subtle tension she had carried for years without naming.

Her body didn't hover, didn't prepare to adjust, didn't brace for emotional shifts that might require immediate recalibration.

She sat fully.

Her hands rested lightly against the surface, her fingers tracing faint grooves in the wood, not searching, not grounding, just noticing—the marks, the scratches, the history embedded into something that had held years without ever asking to be acknowledged.

Ajah entered behind her, closing the door gently, his presence settling into the room without disruption

He didn't expand into the space, didn't attempt to match it.

He let it be what it was, and in doing so, he belonged without needing to claim it, just as he had outside the hospital—present, steady, allowing her to arrive as herself.

Kia glanced at him, then back at her father.

"He's staying for a bit."

James turned then, finally facing them both.

His gaze moved between them, not questioning, not resistant, just taking in what was there, what had shifted, what no longer required explanation.

Then he nodded.

"That's fine."

The simplicity of it moved through the room and settled deeper than permission ever could.

It wasn't approval. It wasn't evaluation. It was acceptance without performance.

Ajah inclined his head slightly.

"I appreciate that."

James gave a small nod in return before turning back to the stove, his movements resuming, steady, uninterrupted.

The room filled with the quiet sound of cooking—oil meeting heat, a soft sizzle, the controlled rhythm of utensils against pan, a man creating consistency in a life that had not always offered it, the same consistency Kia had once mistaken for distance, now understood as devotion without language.

Kia watched him, and for the first time, she didn't just see what he did. She saw what it cost him.

"I used to think you were just... quiet."

James didn't turn.

"I am quiet."

Kia shook her head slightly.

"No," she said. *"You were holding things."*

That made him pause, not long, but enough.

He turned then, leaning slightly against the counter, his arms folding loosely across his chest, his gaze steady on her.

"Somebody had to."

Kia met his eyes, no resistance, no pushback, just understanding that had finally arrived with enough maturity to hold what it meant.

"I know," she said. *"I just didn't understand what that meant for you."*

James studied her for a moment, his posture unchanged, his presence still grounded.

"It meant I didn't always get to feel things when they happened."

The honesty didn't rise. It settled.

Kia felt it in her body before she processed it in her mind, a recognition, not identical, but familiar, aligning with what she had just begun to understand about herself.

"And now?"

James exhaled slowly, his gaze shifting briefly before returning.

"Now I'm learning how to feel them after."

The words carried time, delay, accumulation, emotion deferred until it could be held without breaking the structure that had required it to be postponed.

Kia nodded slowly, because she understood that, in a different way. She had learned to feel everything immediately and then disconnect from it.

He had learned to feel nothing immediately and carry it forward. Different strategies. Same cost.

Ajah shifted slightly beside her, his presence still quiet, his awareness moving between them, not intruding, not interpreting, just witnessing.

Kia turned briefly toward him, then back to her father.

"I went back to see her."

James's gaze sharpened slightly.

"And?"

Kia inhaled slowly, her shoulders settling, her body no longer tightening at the memory.

"We talked."

He waited, and she didn't rush to fill the space.

"I didn't forgive everything."

James nodded once.

"You don't have to."

Kia smiled faintly.

"I know," she said. *"But I let some things go."*

The distinction settled into the room with weight, echoing the decision she had already made, not as a moment, but as a direction she was now walking in.

James studied her for a moment longer, then nodded again, slower, more deliberate.

"That's more than most people do."

The acknowledgment didn't lift her. It grounded her, because it wasn't praise. It was recognition.

The food was ready shortly after, simple, warm, intentional. James placed the plates on the table without ceremony, taking his seat across from Kia, his posture relaxed but present.

They ate, not in silence, but without forcing conversation to fill space that didn't need it.

The rhythm was natural, unperformed, real.

"Where you from?" James asked Ajah after a moment.

Ajah swallowed, then answered evenly.

"Originally London. Studied at the Royal College of Music. I'm at Juilliard now."

James raised an eyebrow slightly.

"Music professor?"

"Yes, sir."

James leaned back slightly, studying him.

"That's not easy to get into."

"No," Ajah replied. *"It's not."*

A pause.

Then—

"You serious about her?"

The question entered the room without warning, but it didn't fracture anything.

It clarified.

Kia's breath caught slightly, not from fear, but from hearing something spoken plainly that had previously lived in the quiet space between understanding and naming.

Ajah didn't hesitate. He met James's gaze directly.

"Yes."

No elaboration. No performance. Just truth.

James held his gaze, measured it, accepted it, then nodded once.

"Alright."

And that was enough.

Kia exhaled softly, something settling in her chest, not because she needed approval, but because the moment had not created tension.

It had held.

After they finished eating, the room softened into something quieter, reflective.

Kia stood near the window, her arms loosely crossed, her gaze moving out toward the city, the same streets she had walked her entire life now carrying a different meaning beneath her awareness.

Ajah stepped beside her, not touching, but close.

"You okay?"

Kia nodded.

"Yeah... I think I am."

She turned toward him, her expression steady, her presence no longer split between past and present.

"This doesn't feel like before."

Ajah studied her.

"No," he agreed. *"It doesn't."*

Kia exhaled slowly, her shoulders relaxing further.

"I'm not trying to fix anything," she said. *"Not with her. Not with him. Not even with me."*

Her voice softened, not from uncertainty, from truth.

"I'm just... letting it be what it is."

Ajah nodded.

"That's where things start to align."

Kia smiled faintly.

"It feels like it."

And standing there, between the life that had shaped her, the love that had steadied her, and the self she was finally allowing to exist without fragmentation, Kia understood something she had been moving toward without fully naming.

She didn't have to choose between where she came from and who she was becoming.

She could hold both.

And in doing that, she wasn't breaking.

She was building.

Chapter Twenty-Six: Loved, Even in the Chaos

The city had found its rhythm again, not the frantic pulse it carried before everything slowed, not the stunned quiet that had unsettled it in 2020, but something in between, something lived-in, something aware of its own fragility and no longer trying to hide it.

The same steadiness Kia had begun to carry within herself now moved through the world around her, not mirroring her, but no longer clashing with her either.

She walked through Central Park with a presence that no longer felt like something she had to maintain. It held on its own.

The path curved beneath her feet in familiar lines, but she noticed the way her body moved across it now, no hesitation in her stride, no subtle tightening in her shoulders, no quiet scanning of the space as if something might interrupt her without warning.

The trees stretched high above her, their branches shifting gently with the wind, leaves catching light in soft, broken fragments that moved across the ground like something alive. The air didn't press against her anymore. It moved with her, around her, through her.

People passed—joggers, couples leaning into one another, children pulling laughter through open space—but none of it crowded her awareness the way it once had. She didn't brace against it. She didn't filter it.

She existed within it, fully, carrying forward the same clarity she had stood in at her father's window, the same quiet decision to no longer fracture herself between where she came from and who she was becoming.

Ahead, the piano sat exactly where it always did, grounded, waiting, not as an object, as a point of return.

Ajah stood beside it, adjusting something near the bench, his movements precise but unforced, his posture relaxed in a way that came from familiarity, not performance.

He didn't look up immediately, but his body registered her, a slight shift in his shoulders, a pause that wasn't interruption—recognition. He always knew.

"You're late," he said lightly, still focused on the keys.

Kia smiled as she approached, her steps unhurried, her presence settling into the space before she even reached him.

"I'm right on time."

Ajah glanced up then, his eyes meeting hers, something warm moving through his expression, not new, not fleeting, established.

"That sounds like something someone late would say."

Kia let out a soft laugh, the sound easy, unmeasured, unprotected.

"Or someone who doesn't rush anymore."

That landed, not as a statement, as truth.

Ajah studied her for a moment longer, his gaze not searching, not questioning, recognizing.

"That too."

Kia sat beside him, close enough to feel his presence without calculating the distance, her body settling naturally into the space, her hands resting loosely in her lap, her breath steady, her spine aligned without effort. She didn't adjust herself to fit the moment. She arrived as she was, and that was enough.

For a moment, neither of them spoke, but the silence didn't stretch. It held, complete.

Ajah turned slightly, his fingers brushing the keys, not playing yet, just feeling the instrument beneath his hands, grounding himself in something tactile, something known.

"You've been different."

Kia tilted her head slightly, her gaze soft but aware.

"So have you."

A small pause, the kind that allows truth to surface without pressure.

"What changed?" he asked.

Kia exhaled slowly, her eyes drifting briefly toward the open space ahead of them, the path, the trees, the movement of people existing without interruption.

Everything that had led her here moved beneath her awareness, not overwhelming, integrated.

"I stopped trying to make sense of everything all at once," she said. *"I stopped trying to fix what already happened."*

Her voice softened, but it didn't lose its structure.

"I let it be what it was... and decided what I wanted to do with it instead."

Ajah listened, fully present, his attention not divided, not anticipating, receiving.

"And what did you decide?"

Kia turned her head slightly, her eyes meeting his, no hesitation, no guarding.

"That I was loved."

The words didn't rise. They settled into the space, into her body, into the truth she had finally stopped resisting.

Ajah's brow shifted slightly, not confusion, attention.

Kia continued.

"Not perfectly. Not consistently. Not always in ways that felt safe or easy. But..." she paused, her breath steady, grounded in what she knew now, *"...it was there."*

Her gaze held his, unshaken.

"My father stayed," she said. *"Even when it cost him. Even when it didn't look like anything was changing."*

A small pause.

"My mother..." she exhaled softly, not retreating from the complexity, *"...she gave me parts of myself I didn't understand until later. Not all of them were easy. But they were real."*

Her voice deepened, not heavier, clearer.

"And you..."

That word shifted something, not fragile, not overwhelming, definitive.

Ajah didn't move, didn't interrupt. He held the space for it.

"You showed me that love doesn't have to feel like something I survive," she said. *"It can feel like something I stand in."*

The air shifted quietly, but completely.

Ajah's hand moved slightly closer, not reaching yet, not claiming, aligning.

"That's what I want it to be," he said quietly.

Kia nodded.

"I know."

A small pause.

Then, without buildup, without performance—

"And I love you."

The words didn't explode. They didn't demand response. They arrived, whole, carrying everything that had led her here without needing to explain it.

Ajah inhaled slowly, the breath settling into him before he released it, his gaze steady, grounded in something that didn't require translation.

"I love you too."

No hesitation. No embellishment. Truth meeting truth.

Kia felt it, not as something overwhelming, as something that fit.

Ajah's hand lifted then, resting gently over hers. The contact was steady, grounded, not pulling, not claiming, just present.

Kia didn't brace. She didn't question. She allowed it.

And in that moment, everything aligned, not perfectly, not without history, not without the echoes of everything that had shaped her, but together, integrated, whole—the same integration she had stepped into with her father, the same release she had chosen with her mother, now no longer separate experiences, but one continuous understanding.

Ajah turned slightly back toward the piano, his fingers settling on the keys, then pausing just long enough to let the moment breathe.

"This one's new."

Kia smiled faintly.

"Play it."

The first notes came slowly, deliberately, not rushing to fill the space, not performing, unfolding.

The sound moved through the air and into her body, not carrying her away, not lifting her out of herself, meeting her exactly where she stood.

Kia closed her eyes, not to escape, to feel.

The music didn't overwhelm her senses. It aligned them—breath, body, memory, presence.

And for the first time in her life, the past did not compete with the present. It existed behind her, within her, but not in control of her.

And in that quiet, steady alignment, Kia understood something that had taken years, pain, distance, and love to fully reveal.

She had not been broken by chaos.

She had been shaped within it.

And now she was no longer surviving it.

She was living beyond it.

Loved.

Even in the chaos.

Epilogue: What She Teaches Forward

The first time someone cried in front of Kia after a performance, she didn't move, not because she didn't care, but because she understood what had just happened.

The woman stood there, hands trembling slightly, fingers curling and uncurling as if her body hadn't yet decided what to do with what had just been released.

Her eyes were wet, but not ashamed, wide in a way that suggested something long-held had finally surfaced without being interrupted, corrected, or contained.

"I didn't know that was still in me," the woman said softly.

Kia held her gaze, not as an actress, not as a performer, but as someone who knew exactly what it meant to carry something for years without language, how it settles into the body, how it reshapes breath, how it becomes normal until something finally reaches it.

"Most things don't leave," Kia replied gently. *"They just wait until we're ready to feel them differently."*

The woman nodded, pressing her lips together as if protecting something newly found, something fragile, but not weak.

Then she stepped back, dissolving into the quiet movement of the theater lobby, her presence blending into others who had come, watched, and left with something they hadn't arrived with.

Kia didn't rush to the next conversation. She didn't shift into performance mode.

She stood there, still, letting the exchange settle into her body the way she had learned to let truth settle, without pushing it away, without reshaping it into something easier to hold.

The stage behind her still carried the echo of what had just happened, not just lines, not just emotion, truth, and that had become her work now, not disappearing into characters, not escaping through performance, but stepping into roles deeply enough to give language to what people carried silently inside themselves.

She no longer stayed in those roles after the curtain fell.

She didn't need to, because she was no longer searching for herself inside them. She had already found herself.

Later that evening, Kia walked through Central Park again, not out of habit, out of alignment.

The city had long since returned to its full voice, horns layering over footsteps, conversations folding into one another, movement without pause, but none of it disrupted her anymore.

The noise didn't invade her.

It existed around her, and she moved within it, whole, carrying herself differently, not guarded, not performing ease, actually at ease.

The piano was there.

It always was.

Ajah sat at the bench, his hands moving across the keys, the music unfolding in a way that no longer felt like performance.

It felt like conversation, with something unseen, but deeply understood.

He looked up as she approached, his gaze softening in recognition that required no announcement.

"You had them tonight," he said.

Kia smiled softly, taking her place beside him, her body settling easily into the space beside his.

"I didn't take them anywhere," she replied. *"I just told the truth."*

Ajah nodded, his fingers brushing the keys lightly, letting the sound linger instead of moving past it too quickly.

"That's what reaches people."

Kia leaned back slightly, her gaze lifting through the branches above them, watching the way light and shadow moved together without conflict.

"I used to think I had to become someone else to be seen," she said.

Ajah glanced at her.

"And now?"

Kia smiled faintly.

"Now I think I just have to be willing to be seen as I am."

The difference was everything.

Ajah's hand found hers easily now, not hesitant, not searching, familiar, grounded.

"That's harder," he said.

Kia nodded.

"It is," she admitted. *"But it lasts longer."*

They sat there, the music moving through the air, through their bodies, not filling emptiness, not covering silence, just existing, just like them.

Across the city, her father sat at the same table, the same quiet presence, the same steady environment he had maintained for years, but something had shifted.

There was less weight in his shoulders now, less tension in the way his hands rested, less pressure in the silence he carried, not because his life had been rewritten, but because something in it had been acknowledged, seen, named, and that mattered.

Kia visited her mother again, not every day, not out of obligation, out of choice.

Their conversations were not perfect. They did not resolve everything.

They did not rewrite the past, but they held truth, and that truth no longer felt like something that could destroy her.

It felt like something she could carry without becoming it.

And somewhere between all of it, the performances, the music, the city, the conversations that no longer avoided what was real, Kia became something she had never been allowed to be before, whole, not because everything had been healed, but because nothing had to be hidden anymore, and that was freedom.

She had been raised in chaos, shaped by it, tested inside it, but she was not defined by it.

She was loved in it, and now she lived beyond it.

Note from the Author:

There are stories we tell for entertainment.

And then there are stories that refuse to let us go until they are spoken.

Loved in Chaos is not a perfect story.

It is not a clean story.

It is not a story where everything is resolved, explained, or tied together in ways that make us feel comfortable.

It is a story about what many of us know intimately—but rarely say out loud.

What it means to grow up in environments where love exists alongside unpredictability.

Where care is present—but not always consistent.

Where survival becomes a language before identity is fully formed.

Kia's story is not about blame.

It is about understanding.

Understanding that two things can exist at the same time:

Love and damage.

Presence and absence.

Care and confusion.

This story may feel close to home in ways you didn't expect.

It explores emotional unpredictability within parent-child relationships, mental health instability within a household, the quiet ways children learn to survive, and the long journey of rebuilding identity after it has been shaped by inconsistency.

If at any point this story stirred something within you—honor that.

Pause when needed.

Return when you are ready.

You are not alone in what you feel.

And you are not broken for having felt it.

This story matters because many of us were loved—but not always in ways that felt safe.

Because many of us learned to survive—before we learned how to be.

Because many of us are still learning how to live beyond what shaped us.

And if this story gave you language…

If it gave you reflection…

If it gave you even a moment of recognition—

Then it has done exactly what it was meant to do.

With truth, with care, and with purpose,

LongTemple

Creator of the Platinum Chocolate Universe

Platinum Chocolate Psychological Sagas

Continue the Journey in the Platinum Chocolate Universe

The **Platinum Chocolate Universe** is a growing collection of interconnected stories celebrating love, resilience, friendship, healing, and the beautifully layered lives of grown people finding their way through the world.

Wherever you begin, every story opens the door to another.

The Ebony M. Elite Series

Friendship. Romance. Sisterhood. And the unforgettable adventure of women rediscovering love later in life.

Start with:

• **Caramel and Steel**

Companion Coloring Book: Caramel and Steel Line Art

Continue with:

• **Searching for Platinum Chocolate**

Companion Coloring Book: Searching for Platinum Chocolate Line Art

Next in the series:

• **When the Chat Paused** — May 1, 2026

The Rhythm Series

A soulful romance shaped by music, faith, ambition, and the kind of love that grows stronger through time.

Start with:

• **Rhythm & Design**

Companion Coloring Book: Rhythm & Design Line Art

Continue with:

• **Rhythm's First Lady**

Companion Coloring Book: Rhythm's First Lady Line Art

Then discover the emotional continuation:

• **When Love Learns to Heal**

Reflective Companion: When the Heart Learns to Heal

The Run Series

A powerful family saga exploring loyalty, survival, love, and the complicated bonds that shape a lifetime.

Start with:

• **Flip & Run**

Companion Coloring Book: Flip & Run Line Art

Next in the series:

• **Just Run** — April 1, 2026

Companion Coloring Book: Just Run Line Art

Stand-Alone Platinum Chocolate Romances

Stories of love, rediscovery, and the courage to begin again.

• **The Colors of Us**

Companion Coloring Book: The Colors of Us Line Art

• **A Heart's Anchor**

Companion Coloring Book: A Heart's Anchor Line Art

• **Cotton Sheets and Velvet Dreams**

Companion Coloring Book: Cotton Sheets and Velvet Dreams Line Art

---

Wherever you begin, the story continues.

www.ingramcontent.com/pod-product-compliance
Lightning Source LLC
LaVergne TN
LVHW020703110826
845149LV00012B/2089

* 9 7 8 1 9 7 2 2 1 7 2 4 5 *